COOKIE!

...and the MOST ANNOYING
GIRL in the WORLD

COOKIE

Developed by Konnie Huq and James Kay

First published in Great Britain in 2020 by
PICCADILLY PRESS
80–81 Wimpole St, London W1G 9RE
Owned by Bonnier Books
Sveavägen 56, Stockholm, Sweden
www.piccadillypress.co.uk
This paperback edition published 2021

This is a work of fiction. Names, places, events and incidents are either
the products of the author's imagination or used fictitiously.
Any resemblance to actual persons, living or dead,
is purely coincidental.

A CIP catalogue record for this book is available
from the British Library.

ISBN: 978-1-84812-863-7
also available as an ebook

1

Typeset by Perfect Bound Ltd
Printed and bound in Great Britain by Clays Ltd, Elcograf S.p.A.

Piccadilly Press is an imprint of Bonnier Books UK
www.bonnierbooks.co.uk

COOKIE!

...and the MOST ANNOYING GIRL in the WORLD

WRITTEN and
ILLUSTRATED by

KONNIE HUQ

Save
the
Planet!

Piccadilly
PRESS

CHAPTER 1

Ugh!

Ugh! Typical! Something just had to go wrong, didn't it? And everything had been going so well since the beginning of term and the whole 'Jake thing'.

I mean, not getting on with Jake almost seems like a blip now!

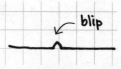

It's weird to think how much I hated Jake at the beginning of the school year. Crazy weird! It's like *that* Jake was a different person from *this* Jake.

Jake then . . .   Jake now . . .

It's so easy to judge a book by its cover . . .

Hmm . . . This book has a boring cover — bet not much happens in it!!

Now that I've got to know him properly he's GREAT and nothing like I thought back in those early days.

HIS DEEDS	MY THOUGHTS	
	THEN	NOW
Giving me some of his Dairy Milk	Ugh! He's trying to show how generous and kind he is	He's generous and kind and shares his Dairy Milk
Bringing homework round when I'm ill off school	Ugh! He's sucking up to my parents to show how studious he is	He's worried I'll get behind at school
Teaching me long words like DEFENESTRATE (to throw out of the window)	He's trying to outsmart me by saying long, cool words	He's helping me expand my vocabulary by saying long, cool words

Me, Jake and Keziah are like a little gang now. Hard to believe, because I've never been in a gang before and also cos I never thought anyone could come between me and Keziah. We've practically been joined at the hip for the last two years.

Before Keziah, I'd always been a bit of a loner. Mum says I was even like that at playgroup. All the other kids loved taking part in group activities, whereas I'd always be doing my own thing at the back of the classroom.

These days, at school, that's harder to do considering I sit right near the front.

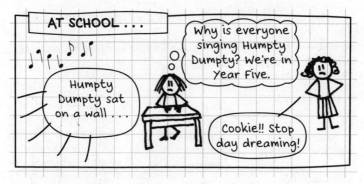

School is actually quite good at the moment. The head teacher, Mrs De Souza, is into science in a big way, so she's got everyone interested in climate

already been implied in the same sentence, like the scorching sun was boiling hot. Well of course it's boiling hot or it wouldn't be scorching!!!

Or calling a mystery mysterious! That's a tautology. Of course mysteries are mysterious. Duh!

Unlike most other people at school, I hardly know my nani cos she lives in Bangladesh. I've only been

there once and although it was for the whole of the summer holidays I was just a baby so I don't even remember it.

Nani is Bengali for a gran that's your mum's mum.

Nani: granny that's your mum's mum	Nana: your mum's dad	Dada: your dad's dad	Dadi: your dad's mum

whole eco-friendly thing too. Can you believe that a one-and-a-half-degree rise in average temperature will have an irreversible effect on our planet?! Loads of different species would be wiped out!

And it would be no good for us humans either. The sea levels would rise, land would be lost and millions of people would be made homeless. How crazy! All because of one and a half degrees. It sounds like nothing!

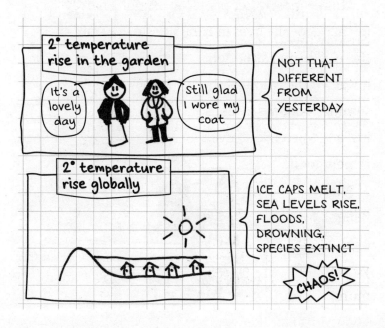

We try to be eco-friendly in everything we do now.

Keziah even cycled over to mine today. Since she got her new bike, her dads let her ride over on her own

at weekends, which is SO good – it's like being an independent grown-up! We can practically spend all of Saturday AND Sunday together. Bliss!

Thank goodness bikes don't have carbon emissions like cars do.

Roubi (my middle sister) has a friend whose dad owns an electric car, which is *also* really good as it doesn't use any petrol. You plug it in to charge as though it's a mobile phone or a tablet. How funny is that?!

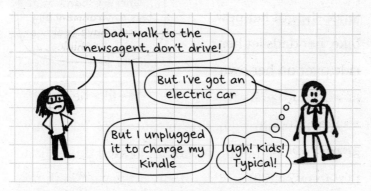

Roubi says it glides along without making any noise and often people don't hear it coming! In the future, all cars will be electric. They'll have to start making fake revving sounds or there'll be a lot of squashed cats on the road!

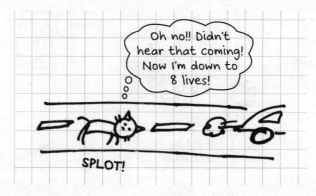

Anyhow, me and Keziah are sitting in the garden discussing what I should do for my upcoming birthday when who should jump over the fence but Bluey, the cat I share with Jake. She's probably getting out the way of next door's lawnmower.

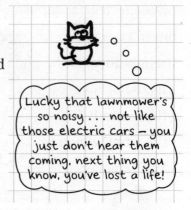

Lucky that lawnmower's so noisy . . . not like those electric cars — you just don't hear them coming, next thing you know, you've lost a life!

As well as sitting beside me at school, Jake is my next-door neighbour. Although I hated this at first, I've come to realise it's actually quite a good thing. It's useful for missed handouts, having someone to chat to on the walk home from school, checking homework and so on. It's also nice to have a friend living so close by.

Oi, can you hear me?

Yeah, can you hear me?

Yeah, it's good being next door, eh?

Yeah . . . saves on the phone bill!

We can hear Jake cutting the grass next door. His parents pay him to do it, and at quite a good rate too. He gets ten pounds for the back lawn and five pounds for the front, which is WAY smaller.

Mum, can I mow the front lawn now?

But you already did it five times this week — how about the back?

Err . . . actually it's OK

If you were going on price per area, he gets a much better deal on the front lawn as it's a tenth of the size!

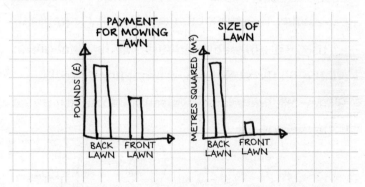

PAYMENT FOR MOWING LAWN

POUNDS (£)

BACK LAWN   FRONT LAWN

SIZE OF LAWN

METRES SQUARED (M²)

BACK LAWN   FRONT LAWN

My parents don't pay me to do anything. I'm just expected to do it all for free. Slave labour if you ask me!

Cookie, we need you to clean inside the chimney for us

What is this? Victorian England?!

After Jake is finished, the three of us end up
sitting in his back garden making friendship chains
with all the freshly cut buttercups and daisies.

'Did you know daisies
and buttercups are
actually weeds?' Keziah
pipes up.

'My gran reckons a
weed is just a plant in the
wrong place,' says Jake. 'It's only a weed if you don't
want it where it is.'

I've never thought of it like that! But I suppose if
a rare orchid grew in the middle of a football pitch
then it kind of would be a weed – you certainly
wouldn't want it there disrupting the game!

'My gran says you can tell if people like butter by
holding a buttercup under their chin and seeing if it
shines yellow,' adds Keziah.

Huh? How do buttercups know if they like butter?

She tries it out on us, confirming we all like butter. I couldn't really add anything to the 'what our grannies say about buttercups and weeds' conversation as my nani lives in Bangladesh and I'm not sure that buttercups and daisies even grow there. Plus, she doesn't speak any English or even have Skype.

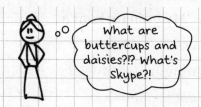

What are buttercups and daisies?!? What's Skype?!

My mum gets long letters from her every now and then but I have no idea of her views on wildflowers . Although I could always add my own views to this conversation . . .

Rubbish? Bit harsh!

'The buttercup test is rubbish!' I declare. They stare at me so I have to back it up.

'It makes it seem like *everyone* loves butter, but surely not everyone in the whole world can!' I continue. 'What about people with a dairy intolerance?'

I knew I was allergic to butter! That lying buttercup!

'Buttercups are so shiny because they're trying to attract insects to pollinate them from a huge distance,' I explain to Jake and Keziah.

After I say it, I instantly realise how square I sound – it's like I just swallowed a textbook!

Luckily it seems to impress Jake, who remarks, 'With knowledge like that you should go on popular TV quiz show *Brainbusters*!' We all laugh.

It's starting to get dark outside and Keziah suggests we go in. Keziah has been scared of the dark ever since I can remember. She still sleeps with a night light on whereas I need pitch-black darkness. The first time I stayed over at her house, I couldn't sleep at all because of her annoying night light.

I can remember watching her Winnie-the-Pooh alarm clock and counting down the hours till morning. I've got used to sleeping at hers since then.

'Nah, let's stay out longer,' says Jake. 'You've got to conquer your fears face-on.'

'Bet, you wouldn't think that if *you* were scared of something,' I say.

'Nothing scares me,' he replies defiantly.

'Everyone's scared of something,' says Keziah. 'Now *please* can we go inside?'

After some protesting by Jake that his room is too messy for visitors and that the beautiful outdoors should be appreciated at night, he finally relents. We sneak past his mum, who is watching the news, and head up to his bedroom. Jake's mum hasn't met Keziah before so if she'd seen us, we'd never have got away – she'd have had Keziah chatting for AGES.

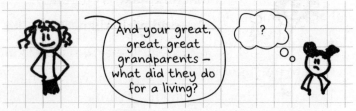

And your great, great, great grandparents – what did they do for a living?

?

As we head upstairs, I notice a load of half-packed suitcases in Jake's parents' bedroom. Keziah asks him if they're going away and Jake tells us that his dad is taking his little brother on a trip to Disneyland as a treat for his birthday. Jake's family are SO cool. We NEVER do stuff like that in our family. I can't imagine getting a trip to Disneyland as a birthday present. That would be off the scale!

DISNEY LAND

'Yay, tickets to Disneyland!'

DISNEY LAND COLOURING BOOK

'Oh . . . it's just a colouring book . . . BAH!'

Jake's bedroom is so much fun to hang out in. It's really cosy with dark walls plastered with posters over every square centimetre, and a soft, thickly carpeted floor. There are loads of gadgets and

gizmos too, including a brand-new Aliana Tiny karaoke machine. Jake is currently obsessed with Aliana Tiny – he has *all* her music and can do *all* the dance moves from *all* her videos.

Jake's a really good dancer but me and Keziah are both rubbish. Unlike most kids our age, we're not really into Aliana Tiny. She's playing Wembley Stadium soon and all the tickets sold out in the FIRST HOUR! They're pretty much like gold dust.

Jake's dad loves taking him to gigs. Maybe he's already snapped up a pair!

Front lawn's great, darling. If you do the back one maybe Daddy will take you to s~ Aliana .

We plonk ourselves down on Jake's bed. Jake has a DOUBLE bed, which is pure luxury. He reckons it's because he has to give up his room if relatives come to stay, but that's probably only once a year so he really *is* getting a good deal. No one else in our class has their OWN double bed. Not even Suzie Ashby.

A double bed wouldn't even *fit* in my room!

Maybe it'll fit if I get rid of my desk and wardrobe?

Double bed sticking out my bedroom door

Keziah looks around. 'Wow! You have so much stuff,' she says. 'All this plastic can't be good for the environment!'

'But it's not single use, like a carrier bag or drinking straw,' Jake protests. 'None of this is going in the bin any time soon.'

Stuff like us Lego bricks are used lots so we're not too bad. It's these pesky single-use things like sweet wrappers you gotta look out for!

At least we're not annoying to step on in bare feet!

'True,' smiles Keziah. 'I've never seen so much stuff though. Your room is like Aladdin's cave!'

'Just birthday presents and bits and pieces that have built up over the years,' he replies.

That reminds me . . . I have to decide what I'm doing for *my* birthday. I never usually do anything but this one's the big 1-0. I'll be an entire decade old! One tenth of a century! Double figures! We all get thinking of a good way to celebrate.

'OMG! Am I taking my whole class to Disneyland?'

'No, Roubi and Nahid didn't want their colouring books!'

'When is it exactly?' asks Jake.

'Two Saturdays' time,' I say.

'Isn't that when Suzie Ashby's birthday party is?' Jake replies. 'Apparently she's inviting everyone in the class. I heard her telling Alison Denbigh. She reckons she's even getting a party planner.'

Keziah bursts out laughing. 'What? That's a bit grand, isn't it!? Where's she holding it? The Ritz?!'

Ugh! Suzie Ashby is having a party with the whole class at the Ritz – on MY birthday. How can I compete with that? I'll have to think of something . . . and fast . . .

CHAPTER 2

The Worst Birthday Ever!

Suzie Ashby is stealing my birthday. There are 364 other days in the year on which she could've had her party. But oh no, she has to go and choose the one day of the year that is MY BIRTHDAY. What are the odds?

$$\text{Probability of Suzie's party being on my birthday} = \frac{1}{365} \left(\frac{\text{no. of days my birthday is on}}{\text{no. of days Suzie could have her party on}} \right)$$

I spend the whole of the next day racking my brains about how to celebrate my birthday. I'd usually be quite happy just going to the cinema with Keziah and Jake and getting pizza afterwards, but Suzie was setting the bar really high here. How could I settle for pizza when she was throwing a BIG soirée?

Was she really gonna invite the whole class? That's thirty kids! To be honest, I could imagine her inviting the whole *year group* – all sixty of us! And not because she's kind or generous but because she's a show-off. She just wants to look good in front of everyone.

It's all about image with Suzie . . .

I'm going to have to come up with something brilliant now. Thanks a bunch, Suze!

ad suggests having a few people over to our house for party games.

'I'm not turning five,' I protest. 'We can't play pass the parcel or pin the tail on the donkey!'

Nothing wrong with pass the parcel . . . I'm a classic!

What was he thinking?!

Party games indeed. I sit in the kitchen pondering the matter while Roubi makes herself some toast and Dad leafs through the local paper.

'How about a bouncy castle?' he suggests. 'There's a 40 per cent off voucher for bouncy castle hire in here.'

My bouncy castle has already deflated and people will be here soon. I knew there'd be a catch with 40% off!

To be honest, I do still love a good bouncy castle but it is maybe a bit babyish for my *tenth* birthday party.

'Ugh! Next you'll be suggesting I go to a soft play centre,' I reply sarcastically. 'I'm over halfway to becoming an adult now, you do realise? I need to celebrate like an adult.'

'What?' chuckles Dad. 'Going to a disco till past midnight? I don't think so!'

Well, I didn't mean celebrate like an *actual* adult. I meant some sort of outing or themed party as opposed to musical bumps and jammy dodgers. When Nahid (my eldest sister) finished high school, her whole year group had a leavers' 'sun, sea and surf' party. Everyone wore beach dresses and Hawaiian shirts and there were even fake palm trees, a barbecue and fruit cocktails. Apparently

they limbo-danced and played volleyball.

THAT'S IT! I'll do that!

But it's not summer, so everyone would freeze . . .

21

Waaah! At this rate Keziah and Jake would be the only two coming – and they're only coming cos I made them promise me they would. I mean, they'd be real traitors if they went to Suzie's over mine. I reckon Axel would probably come as well. Axel sits next to Keziah at school. We didn't really know him at the beginning of term and thought he was a bit strange, but actually he's really funny. He's a good judge of character so he definitely wouldn't want to go to Suzie's.

Roubi sits down at the table to eat her toast as Dad chucks his newspaper out.

'This paper is full of adverts and no news!' he declares, throwing it into the bin.

'Recycling, Dad,' I sigh. 'Put it in the recycling bin!' He always puts paper and plastics in the main bin. When will he learn?

'You should have a "Save the Planet" party, Cookie,' suggests Roubi. 'That would be really fun and a worthwhile theme too. Better still, you're genuinely into it.'

Genius! Why didn't I think of that? I'll have a 'Save the Planet' party. Everything will be sustainable – no plastic whatsoever. Paper plates, paper cups, paper drinking straws and even paper decorations! Instead of goody bags I'll give out packets of seeds so people can plant more trees!!

This idea is coming together already and we've only just thought of it! All the food would be vegetarian – meat is a real eco no-no. Luckily, I don't eat pork anyway so I'm part of the way there.

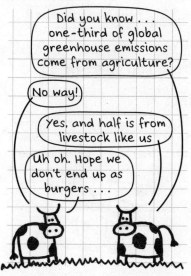

23

I could even
encourage people
to walk or cycle
to the party, and I
could give all the
leftover food to
the homeless.

The invites could be emailed out so as not to
waste paper. Although I'm not allowed on any social
media, our school is really
into science and technology
so it has its very own email
network. I can't wait to
message everyone about my
party – there'll be such a buzz!

Yippee! My first proper birthday party! Up until
now I've always just done low-key stuff with a few
people. Times are changing!

At school on Monday morning, there's a bright
pink envelope on everyone's desks.

I look down at mine. On
the front it says 'Cookie
Haque' in large swirly
gold writing.

Ugh! I know exactly what this is. I pull out a glossy pink plastic invitation and a multicoloured

cloud of glitter explodes all over my desk. I open it

and am greeted by a pop-up image of Suzie grinning with the words 'Happy Birthday to Me!' printed underneath. Ewww!

I scan the room for Suzie.

'Hey, Suzie,' I yell in her direction. 'What a coincidence – my party is on the same day as your party. We're birthday buddies!'

Suzie turns as pink as her invite. 'My birthday's *actually* on the Wednesday before so I'm *actually*

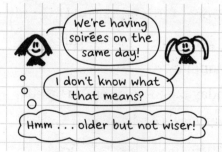

older than you and we're not *actually* birthday buddies,' she says.

'How come your party is on the same day as mine anyway? *I* didn't get an invite!'

'My birthday is actually *on* that day and my invites are going out by email as it's more environmentally friendly,' I say smugly. 'You see, it's a "Save the Planet" party.'

Suzie turns even pinker and splutters, 'Errr, yeah, I mean no, I mean . . . no way, so is mine.'

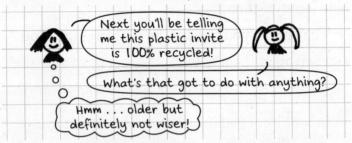

There is NOTHING on her invite saying 'Save the Planet' party. She's just made it up on the spot to compete with me!

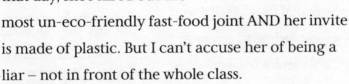

Her birthday isn't even on that day, she's hired out the most un-eco-friendly fast-food joint AND her invite is made of plastic. But I can't accuse her of being a liar – not in front of the whole class.

I mean, Suzie is the least environmentally friendly person I can think of! Everything about her says *destroy* the planet, not *save* it.

At lunch, I report the whole thing to my dinner lady buddy, Selina.

'I'll come to your party,' she reassures me, 'and I can bring my grandchildren if you need to make up the numbers. I have forty-seven in total. Or is it forty-eight?'

She probably would as well . . .

Selina assures me that Suzie will get a very small portion of chips today and I giggle as I head over to Keziah and Axel, who are already sitting down at a table, munching on their lunch and chatting away.

Turns out Axel hasn't even been *invited* to Suzie's party. She can be SO mean sometimes. She's invited every other person in the class. She'd claim it was an oversight if anyone pulled her up on it, but I know that she didn't invite Axel 'I always look at the

floor' Kahn on purpose because he's not very popular. Axel doesn't seem to mind in the slightest, though.

Thank goodness I wasn't invited! At least I don't need to make up an excuse to get out of it!

Well, Axel is welcome at *my* party, so that's four definites – including me.

Party! Yay! Woo!

Is it just us?

After we finish our food, we go around telling everyone about the party. We even get some good eco-conscious party suggestions . . .

PARTY IDEAS

1. No palm oil in food (a lot of palm oil production destroys rainforests and contributes to greenhouse gases and emissions)

You can use me if I'm sustainable!

2. All party clothes should be natural fibres, not synthetics (which aren't biodegradable)

100% natural

Oh yeah!

3. Candlelight (to save electricity) but may cause a fire (uh oh!) so maybe not!

I'm fiery!

I'm loving everyone's input. If people feel they've helped to contribute, they'll definitely want to come. Maybe I'll even get the same number of guests as Suzie.

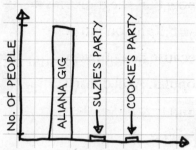

By the end of lunchtime, I'm starting to think I might even beat her. I tell Tayo Akinola he can DJ and he says, of his own accord, that he can try and pick music that's environmentally friendly!!! I have no idea what he means by that (maybe music about nature and animals?!) but I

SOMEWHERE OVER THE RAINBOW!

go along with it anyhow as it seems to make him happy!

I'm SO excited about the whole thing. When I get home, I run up to Roubi's room and ask her to help me design an invite. I'm thinking that I could maybe even write on it that for every acceptance

I get, a donation will go to Friends of the Earth or some other environmental charity. But maybe that would be weird – like I was trying to guilt-trip people into coming.

Come to my party! If you don't, the planet will die! We'll all die!!

Where would I hold it? I haven't even thought about a venue yet. In the local park? Or better still, the community nature reserve? But it might be too cold or too rainy. The back garden would probably be best. Still close to nature but we could always go inside if we needed to. I run downstairs to check with Mum, who's busily scrawling something on the kitchen calendar. She's not really listening to me and is just pretending to, the way mums sometimes do . . .

Are you listening, Mum?

Yes . . .

Of course not . . .

Me: 'So I think I'll have my party here.'

Mum: 'Oh, OK.'

Me: 'For my birthday.'

Mum: 'Oh, OK.'

Me: 'Great. Saturday.'

Mum: 'OK.'

Me: 'That's the Saturday after next.'

Mum: 'OK.'

Me: 'Saturday the 16th.'

*Mum: 'Huh? Saturday the 16th? Oh . . . no, that's
not OK. Sorry! We're going to Uncle Mehdi's that day.
They're having a big celebration at their house and
your cousin's cousin's brother-in-law's cousin's cousin
and their family are visiting from Canada so we have
to go.'*

*Me: 'Ugh! But that's my birthday! Don't you even
know when your own daughter's birthday is?!'*

*Mum: 'Sorry, Roubi, I'm thinking about something
else right now!'*

*Me: 'Urghhhhh! I'm Cookie!!! Don't you even know
who your own daughter is?!'*

Mum: 'That's nice.'

No. Way. So unfair. No birthday party for me on my
tenth birthday. The big 1-0! A decade old! A tenth of
a century! Double figures! Typical. Everyone will
go and have fun at Suzie's now and, worse still, I'll
be stuck at Uncle Mehdi's. Great. Just great. Worst
birthday ever.

CHAPTER 3

The Best Birthday Ever!

There are 364 other days in the year on which Uncle Mehdi could have had his party. But oh no, he has to go and choose the one day that is MY BIRTHDAY. Keziah suggests I have my party on the Sunday instead but I've gone right off the idea now. Besides, I don't want Suzie to think I've changed the date because I'm worried about the competition.

Typical! She's changed the date because she's worried about the competition!

I also don't want people going to both parties and comparing mine to hers. That would be way too stressful. Anyhow, big parties aren't really my thing, which is why I never have them . . .

POSSIBLE PROBLEMS:

The pressure is just too much. I like going to other people's parties but holding my own . . . no thanks! I'll go to the cinema with Keziah and Jake on the Sunday instead. We could even get pizza afterwards. Much less stressful.

Why didn't I think of that before?

'Pizza and cinema sounds good,' says Jake.

'And if you change your mind we can still invite the rest of the class,' laughs Keziah.

'What d'you want as a present?' asks Jake.

'You guys don't need to get me anything – your friendship is enough!' I say, giving Keziah a massive bear hug.

'Awww, shucks!' she says, planting a huge kiss on my cheek.

'But what are you getting from your parents?' Jake asks.

'I've been dropping loads of hints that I want a bike,' I reply, 'but I'm not sure that I've made it clear enough.'

Cookie, can you post a letter for me?

Ugh . . . the postbox is miles away. If only I had a bike . . .

Cookie, can you take the rubbish out?

Ugh . . . to the outdoor bin? If only I had a bike . . .

Cookie, can you pass the remote control?

If only I had a bike . . .

'I bet they've got you one,' says Jake. 'They totally picked up on you wanting a pet when they got you your fish.'

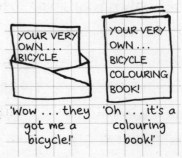

YOUR VERY OWN . . . BICYCLE

'Wow . . . they got me a bicycle!'

YOUR VERY OWN . . . BICYCLE COLOURING BOOK!

'Oh . . . it's a colouring book!'

Suzie's been telling everyone that she's getting Aliana Tiny tickets from her parents. Most of our class are really into Aliana, especially Jake. She should be so lucky though. Apparently those tickets are now selling for £300 each on the Internet.

Unless, of course, her parents got them the minute they went on sale, which, thinking about it, they probably would have done. Knowing Suzie, they're most likely VIP tickets. Her parents have connections. They always seem to know someone who knows someone who can pull strings for just about anything.

Not only is Suzie going to have an amazing party with the whole class (well, minus Keziah, Jake and Axel), but she's probably going to be in a private box at Wembley with cushioned seats and pot plants.

Anyway, what am I so bothered about? I don't even like Aliana Tiny. Although her songs are really catchy, the lyrics are *soooo* rubbish.

Be who you am . . .
Am who you be . . .
Say what you like . . .
You'll never be me . . .

They don't even make sense . . . Am who you be?!! What does that even mean?!!!

Am who you be

No, I'll be who I am, thanks

Same thing!

No, the first one doesn't make grammatical sense!

I don't ask for much in life. I wouldn't be fussed about having a box at an Aliana Tiny gig. I'm not even having a party. But pleeeeaaassseee can I get a bicycle?!!!

The morning of my birthday, I'm up and out of bed by 6.30 a.m. I glance in the mirror and actually think I look a bit older and more mature. I'm not sure why but I reckon my face has lost a bit of puppy fat in the night or something.

Wow, I look so much older . . . Oh, that's a picture of Roubi!

Everyone else is still asleep. I go downstairs and there on the kitchen table is an envelope with my name on it. No bike in view anywhere, but then again, it's not an easy present to wrap so maybe it's in the shed or something. I open my birthday card. On the front, there's a picture of a bike and underneath it says 'Have a *wheelie* good birthday'. Well, I would if I had a bike . . .

Inside is a gift voucher for twenty-five pounds towards a bike from Mike's Bikes (our local bike shop) and a complimentary bell of my choosing, costing four pounds or under. Can you even get a bell for four pounds or under?!

Roubi comes downstairs and gives me a present from her and Nahid (my other sister who's at uni). It's an Aliana Tiny piggy bank so I can start saving up for the bike! Thanks, guys!

Great. No bike. No party. Uncle Mehdi's instead. Worst birthday ever.

Uncle Mehdi is my dad's cousin. He has two daughters – Amaya who is eighteen months and Aaliyah who is three years old – and they are both utterly adorable. They look up to me like the older sister they never had.

Although I guess one of them does have an older sister. Not one as cool as me though . . .

Today, as per usual, Aaliyah follows me about everywhere and Amaya just loves being cuddled by me. I spend most of my time at my uncle's playing with them so I don't have to speak to anyone else, as I'm not in the mood for chit-chat. My uncle's favourite topics of conversation are the weather (whether it's good or bad), the traffic (whether it's good or bad) and the government (whether they're good or bad). BORING!

Meanwhile, all my other relatives keep going on about how much I've grown. Why do adults continually find this so fascinating? Yep!! Well done!! I've grown! Of course I have! I'm a child – it's what children do! We grow!! You haven't seen me in ages! It'd be a bit weird if I hadn't grown, wouldn't it?! It's how the human body works! We

ingest food and we grow!!! You grew too. That's why you're a grown-up . . . you grew up. The clue is in the title. GROWN. UP. Imagine if I was still the same size as five years ago?

I am ten, honest . . . I just haven't grown in the last five years!

After we've eaten, Amaya and Aaliyah are whisked away to bed. I wander into my uncle's study and log on to the computer. Suzie's party would be finishing round about now. I pull up her Instagram feed to see if she's posted anything. Eww! It seems this was the event of the century. She's practically live-streaming the whole party. How can she be entertaining anyone if she's been posing for pictures every five seconds?!!

Is there any food here?

We've been here for three hours!

Hang on, just taking a selfie!

NO TO PLASTIC!!

SAVE THE PLANET

Plastic sign

Nylon top

Nothing about this party says 'Save the Planet'. There's enough plastic there to rival a Barbie factory.

There's a huge plastic banner hung from the ceiling across the wall and balloons everywhere.

39

Suzie and everyone else are guzzling from plastic cups and plastic bottles with plastic straws and eating off plastic plates. I can even see plastic goody bags lined up on the table in the background of one photo. Huh?! There's a goody bag with *my* name on it! Awww! That's nice! Perhaps she'll save it for me. Poor Suzie! Maybe I've been a bit hard on her. At least she's trying to grasp the concept of saving the planet.

Which planet are we saving, again?

I smile to myself as I scroll through more photos, then do a double-take as I look at one . . . hang on . . . it can't be! I feel sick and betrayed. No! It can't be! Can it? It is. There in the corner of one of the pictures are Jake and Keziah!!!!

How could they go to Suzie's party without me?
They promised they wouldn't! TRAITORS!!!! I feel
sick.

'Knock, knock, knock! Where is she?' comes
Uncle Mehdi's voice at that same moment. 'Little
Miss Birthday Girl! I've hardly seen you today!'

That's because I've been avoiding everyone, I
think, as he enters the study. Please not now! I've
just been dealt a terrible blow.

'Did you guys get here OK? Traffic so bad,
and weather so
awful. I blame
the government!
Wow, Cookie!
You've grown.'

Before I can
reply 'Really?
How strange,' he
introduces me
to my cousin's

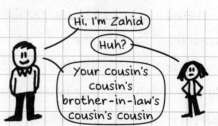

cousin's brother-in-law's cousin's cousin, Zahid.

'Hi Cookie, nice to meet you,' says Zahid. 'Happy
birthday! These are for you – I got them through
my work!'

'Amaya and Aaliyah are too young for them, even though she's their favourite,' says Uncle Mehdi.

I have no idea what on earth they're talking about, but then I open the envelope . . .

No way!

Noooooo waaaaaay!

NOOOOOOOO WAAAAAAAAAAAAAAYYYY!!!!

TWO TICKETS TO THE ALIANA TINY GIG! UNBELIEVABLE!!!!!!!

'Thanks so much! I love Aliana Tiny!' I declare. 'She's my absolute favourite!'

And all of a sudden, she was! I start singing, 'Be who you am, am who you be, say what you like, you'll never be me!' surprising even myself.

Wait till everyone finds out I have two tickets to the Aliana Tiny concert! I'll be the envy of the school. Maybe not such a bad birthday after all!

CHAPTER 4

Traitors!

The next morning, I realise that Suzie Ashby can't have got Aliana Tiny tickets for her birthday because if she had done, she would definitely have posted about it on Instagram. She'd put pictures of all her other hundreds of presents up there. I'm still annoyed at the fact that she stole my 'Save the Planet' party idea and that she didn't invite poor Axel to it. I decide to email her right away to give her a taste of her own medicine.

I get Mum to log me on to the school network.

To: Suzie Ashby
From: Cookie Haque
Time: 09.27

Hey babes [Suzie], or should I say birthday buddy! [Sucking up to Suzie while also reminding her we are the same star sign]. Just wanted to say sooooooooo [so] totes [totally] annoying that I had to miss out on your soirée [party]. As you know, I had to meet my cuz [cousin] who jet-setted [flew] in for my birthday [well, four days that happened to include my birthday] so I totes [totally] even had to ditch [cancel] my own do [party]. Bummer [so annoying]. What I couldn't tell you before [cos I didn't know] as it was top secret [like I said, I didn't know] was that my cuz [well, my cousin's cousin's brother-in-law's cousin's cousin to be precise] knows Aliana [works for the same firm of accountants that do her accounts]. He's Canadian like her [he's Canadian like her]. So as you have tickets [I know you don't] and I have tickets [I do, hah hah], maybe we should all go together??!!

Laters [that's it for now]

44

Cookie XXXXXXX [lots of kisses to curry favour]

It's not long before I get a reply . . .

To: Cookie Haque

From: Suzie Ashby

Time: 09.43

Angel pie [me],

Really missed you yesterday 😔 [don't really care you weren't there but I know you have Aliana tickets 😍]. Wasn't the same without you [like I said, don't really care you weren't there but I know you have Aliana tickets 😍]. Total mix up with my birthday list means I didn't get any Altix [Aliana tickets?!!!] after all 😔 [my parents couldn't get hold of any despite pulling all possible strings 😠]. Totes amazing you're going 😍 [totally jealous and annoyed you're going and I'm not 😩]. If you need anyone to go with, I'd be more than happy to . . . 😁 [YOU MUST TAKE ME WITH YOU!!! 🙏]

Huge love [not really huge love but please take me with you!!!]

Suzie XXXXX [lots of kisses to curry favour]

P.S. I've saved your party bag for you [bribery to curry

even more favour]

OMG!! The power of Aliana tickets. I feel a bit bad, but then again Suzie's done so much mean stuff over the years – this seems minor in comparison. I play hard to get and wait a whole hour before sending a reply.

To: Suzie Ashby
From: Cookie Haque
Time: 10.43

Babycakes [Suzie],

Not sure who I'm taking yet 🤔 but will defs bear you in mind. [Not sure who I'm taking yet and will definitely make the most of this opportunity for you to beg me for it 🙏].

See ya tomoz 😘 [see you tomorrow 😐]

Cookie xxx [small kisses to treat you mean and keep you keen]

Suzie replies instantly . . .

To: Cookie Haque
From: Suzie Ashby
Time: 10.44

OK gorgeous 😍 [OK]
Love ya Xxx. 🖤🖤 😘 [Don't really but I WANT
THOSE TICKETS!!]

Suzie is ALL OVER ME. This is great! I decide to send
out another email to the whole class to spread the
word that I have Aliana tickets!

To: Undisclosed recipients [Everyone in Sparrowhawk
class]
From: Cookie Haque
Time: 11.09

Hey y'all,
Hope you're having an AMAZING weekend.
Just wondering whether anyone else is going to the
Aliana 'Be Who You Am' exclusive UK gig? Thought it
might be fun to go as a group if so . . .

Let me know

Love Cookie Xxxxx

I know that no one else is going to the gig but this is good PR for me. The 'Be Who You Am Tour' is Aliana's first long-awaited global tour and has been in the news for ages and now I'm a part of its UK leg!!

Public relations — Kind of like advertising my brand (or rather, me!)

I get an instant reply! I knew this would get everyone excited. I click it open . . .

To: Cookie Haque

From: Manjula Mannan [Mrs Mannan]

Time: 11.11

Sorry, Cookie, I am busy that day. [Sorry but I don't want to go out with a bunch of kids to an Aliana Tiny gig on my day off. The lyrics are catchy though!]
Best regards, [Go away now!]
Mrs Mannan [Manjula apparently?! It's funny that teachers have first names]

Oops! I forgot to delete Mrs Mannan from the class list. Thank goodness she's busy! Phew!

Luckily she's not the only person who replies.

Loads of the class get in touch to find out more or
to say how lucky I am. Even Axel emails back . . .

To: Cookie Haque
From: Axel Kahn
Time: 11.29

Hi . . . Are you serious?
Axel

I love Axel's weirdness. I giggle to myself but then
an email from Keziah pops up and I remember
we're supposed to be going to the cinema today
with Jake. No thanks! Traitors!

To: Cookie Haque
From: Keziah King
Time: 11.31

Hey Cook . . .
Aliana?!! Ha, ha! No way!!
Call you after lunch to find out
more!!!
KK Xxxx

I know the way to Cookie's heart – I'll use our special pet names and sign off with KK!

P.S. Shall I bike to yours before the cinema? Could come at around 2.30 or 3ish?

KK is my affectionate nickname for Keziah that I used a lot in the early days. I haven't called her KK at all this term. Maybe she's feeling guilty about going to Suzie's yesterday?

I quickly type out a reply . . .

To: Keziah King
From: Cookie Haque
Time: 11.34

I'm busy today now so let Jake know that I'm cancelling the cinema trip. Feel free to go without me as you seem to be quite good at that!

Best regards, [go away now]
Cookie [no kisses to show that I'm angry]

Keziah tries to
call me but I make
Roubi say that
I've gone out. Ha!
Who's laughing

now, I think, looking at my gold embossed Aliana tickets.

It's really rainy on Monday morning and as we all queue outside school eager to get into the dry, I can tell that word has got around about my birthday gift. It feels like everyone is  looking at me knowingly. Random students say hi and everyone's being extra nice to me.

'Hey babe, missed you Saturday!' Suzie calls out to me in front of the whole class. 'Remind me to give you your goody bag later'. Her best friend 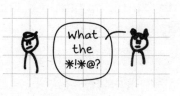 Alison Denbigh (who lives for Suzie's approval) looks baffled, as do Jake and Keziah.

Maybe I *should* take Suzie to the gig? I can't take Jake anymore. Traitor! He emailed me yesterday after I cancelled the cinema trip to say he didn't understand why I was annoyed and that of course  he and Keziah wouldn't have gone to Suzie's party

51

if my party had gone ahead. Ugh! 'He and Keziah'!
What are they now? A married couple?

I bet they went to the cinema without me too.
TRAITORS!

I wish they'd open the school doors – we're
getting pretty wet out here. Suddenly, a loud voice
bellows across the playground, interrupting my
thoughts. I look up to see the new supply teacher,
Mrs Edmonds, shouting at Martha Masters because
she's dropped a tissue. Martha is in our year in
Kestrel class. She's really sweet and isn't the type to
drop litter on purpose. Edmonds orders her to do
twenty press-ups as we all begin to shuffle in. Poor
Martha! Worse still, it's
now started bucketing
down
with rain. Talk about
strict! That was a bit

Hurry up,
Martha, we
used to do this
one-handed in
our platoon!

much really. I can see others thinking the same
thing.

I hear Edmonds used to be in the army, which
would totally figure.

During class, I glare at Jake and Keziah while
Mrs Mannan reads us some of *The Witches*, the

Roald Dahl book we're currently studying. It's a bit creepy. In fact, Axel isn't even allowed to

listen to it because his mum thinks it's too scary for him, so he has to sit outside the classroom reading something else instead, even though he's not at all scared of it. Bit ridiculous if you ask me.

Afterwards, we have a group discussion on fear and we all have to tell the class something we're scared of.

'Mrs Edmonds!' shouts Tayo, and everyone laughs.

Mrs Mannan works her way round the room while I think hard about what it is that frightens me.

Keziah says she's scared of the dark, Axel can't bear heights, Suzie is terrified of bacteria and Alison Denbigh's fear is ghosts. I mean, who believes in ghosts?! Total nonsense!

In the end, I say swans as I do kind of have a phobia of them. Thinking back over the last couple of days, I wonder whether Roubi was right when she once said I have FOMO – a Fear Of Missing Out. Was that why I didn't want Jake and Keziah to go to Suzie's party without me? And did it explain why I now wanted to go to the Aliana gig even though I'm not a fan? I put the thought out of my mind as it was Jake's turn to answer. He declares to the class that he 'honestly isn't scared of anything'. Yawn!

'Everyone's scared of something,' says Mrs Mannan, speaking the most sense I've heard from her in ages.

'Certainly not scared of being a traitor,' I whisper under my breath.

'We didn't know you wouldn't want us to go to Suzie's once you'd cancelled your *own* party', he says exasperatedly. 'I only went to get out of the house as my brother was annoying me.'

His brother was annoying him?!! What a liar! Not scared of anything?! Double liar! I'm going to find out what he's scared of – I'll make sure of it.

CHAPTER 5

Muddy Heap

'**Are** you scared of your little brother or something, Jake?' I taunt him in the playground at lunchtime. 'Is that what your fear is?!' Does he seriously think I'd believe he went to Suzie's party because he wanted to escape a seven-year-old?! Hardly something to be afraid of, or whatever it is he claims. It's one thing to be a traitor but another to be a liar as well.

Jake looks like he's about to cry. Maybe he *is* scared of his brother? Maybe his brother's a bully?!

I feel a bit bad but I'm not letting this go. I still can't believe that he and Keziah actually thought I wouldn't find out about them going to Suzie's party behind my back.

'What were you playing at?' I ask. 'Did you have to hide in the background every time a photo was taken so you wouldn't be rumbled? Did you really think you'd get away with it?!'

'We didn't think we were getting away with anything,' protests Keziah. 'We thought you were OK with us going, especially as you'd cancelled your own party. *And* you said you were busy!'

Busy?! Busy at Uncle Mehdi's being told that I'd grown, and being informed of traffic and weather conditions. So very busy! (Although admittedly I did get my highly sought-after birthday present, heh, heh, heh!) Hang on a second . . . on the subject of birthday presents, I know I'd told Keziah and Jake not to get me anything, but they actually didn't get me *anything*. Not a single thing. Nothing. I thought they might have at least got me a little

Nothing to see here!

Empty box

something. NOT EVEN A CARD!!! ABSOLUTELY NOTHING!!

Even Axel got me a card, although it *was* in German. Axel's parents are German and he says that it was all he could find knocking around his house. He even brought it in on the Friday so I had it for my birthday on the Saturday. I was really surprised. For someone who looks at the floor 99.9 per cent of the time, it was quite a charming touch.

It had '*Glückwunsch zu ihrem baby*' written on it. '*Glückwunsch zu ihrem baby*'? Maybe that means 'Happy birthday baby!' in German?

Dear Cookie

Happy birthday
GLÜCKWUNSCH ZU IHREM BABY
Love
Axel x

x x

Roubi put it into Google Translate and turns out it actually means 'Congratulations on your new baby'. He probably thought I wouldn't realise.

As long as the picture on the front of the card isn't a baby but something else, it can pass as a birthday card . . .

True!

Thanks for my new baby card!

I was too busy looking at the floor to look at the message inside!

I don't care though. At least he got me a card – it's the thought that counts.

'Even Axel is a better friend!' I shout. 'He didn't go to Suzie's AND he got me a card. You two didn't get me anything!'

'Honestly, Cookie, sometimes you're so crazy,' says Jake, rolling his eyes and walking off.

Keziah giggles. 'You are a little . . . but that's why I like you!'

She then points out that she'd sent me an e-card (oops – forgot about that!). She thought I'd prefer it as it's more eco-friendly and I'm so into saving the planet. She does have a point, I guess.

'Look,' says Keziah, 'me and Jake went to the shops to get you a present on the Saturday. We couldn't decide on anything good so we thought we'd treat you to your cinema ticket on the Sunday, as well as popcorn and snacks.'

'Oh,' I reply. 'That would have been a really cool present.'

'Anyway, after we were done, Jake said he really didn't want to go home because of his little brother,' Keziah continues. 'He insisted we go to Suzie's. He was acting really weird, like he was gonna cry or something, so I went with him.'

I know Keziah is telling the truth. She's terrible at lying!

KEZIAH TELLING THE TRUTH

Jake didn't want to go home so we went to Suzie's . . .

KEZIAH LYING

Jake didn't want to go home so we went to Suzie's . . .

We both think Jake's story is a bit fishy. Wasn't his brother supposed to be going to Disneyland with his dad? Surely they couldn't have gone and come back already? How did they clear it with the school? Keziah is sure she's seen his brother around recently. I haven't though, and I do live next door to them, so who knows? I haven't really been over to Jake's lately – he's been a bit distant. It's so strange.

Edmonds is back on lunch duty. Jake has wandered off to the other side of the playground and is sat chatting to Axel under the big tree. Axel often sits there alone on his log. Whereas everyone else wants to hang out with their friends at lunchtime, Axel doesn't seem to mind doing his own thing.

I wish I could be more like that. It must be my FOMO stopping me!

Keziah and I start to walk towards Axel's log.

'Are you OK?' I ask Jake, feeling a bit guilty.

He says he's fine but I get the feeling he's about to say something else when Suzie bounds over with Alison in tow.

'Hey babe!' she says, giving me a huge hug while Keziah and Jake look on, utterly confused. 'So, I didn't want to squash your goody bag by bringing it into school in my backpack and then I had a great idea . . . Why don't you come over to mine on Saturday and I'll give it to you then?!'

Huh?!

I'm always intrigued by other people's houses. I've never been to Suzie's house before but I've seen bits of it on Instagram. Her bedroom looks massive. Although I'm not really friends with Suzie, I'd still love to see her house in real life.

'Yeah, definitely,' I say without even having to think about it.

'Great, babe, it's a date,' she says, flashing me a dazzling grin.

Mwah ha ha . . . she thinks I like her but I just like the ticket!

Alison Denbigh looks like she's been fatally wounded and starts protesting that they're supposed to be going to some gymnastics gala on Saturday. Suzie rolls her eyes and turns to me apologetically.

'Excuse me for a moment, please,' she says, and then she and Alison start having a massive row like a married couple.

We're over

Yes, I agree

What's going on?! Suzie is arguing with Alison over *me* and I'm . . .

enjoying it! I don't know why but I kind of *do* want to be Suzie's friend at the moment. She did save me my goody bag *and* she was being really nice to me, unlike my traitor friends. Maybe Suzie is the breath of fresh air I need right now. It feels nice to have someone who *wants* to hang out with me.

'Suzie's party bags are really brilliant,' says Keziah. 'Mine had a plastic ink pad and stamps, some plastic alphabet fridge magnets, some plastic

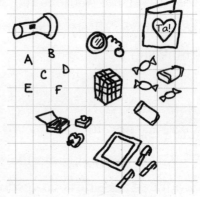

dry-wipe neon marker pens and mini dry-wipe marker board . . . oh yeah, and a plastic "thank you for coming to my Save the Planet party" card.'

'So much for saving the planet!' says Jake. 'I've never seen so much plastic in my entire life.'

What about in your bedroom? TRAITOR!

I immediately jump in to defend my new friend, Suzie, who luckily hasn't overheard as she's still busy arguing with Alison.

'Well, I'm sure that didn't stop *you* taking a goody bag,' I snap.

'What are you now? Best buddies?' Jake sneers.

'You're the one who went to her party,' I reply. 'Whereas she's extending me hospitality, you just seem to make up lies and excuses these days so I don't come over to yours. *And* you live next door *and* Bluey is half my cat. Talking of which, where are my visiting rights?'

'Visiting rights?! What is this? A divorce?!' says Jake, tears forming in the corners of his eyes.

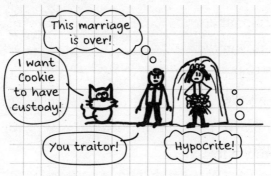

I'm a bit taken aback. Why is he acting so weird?

Keziah tries to intervene. 'Hey, let's all calm down.'

Meanwhile, Suzie and Alison are far from calm. They're still arguing loudly over anything and everything.

'See!' says Jake. 'You're even causing *them* to argue, Cookie! We all know Suzie only invited you over to hers because she wants your spare gig ticket.'

HOW RUDE!

'Has it ever crossed your mind that maybe I'm a nice person and she WANTS to hang out with me?!' I yell. 'Maybe she actually LIKES me. Maybe she knows I'd make a LOYAL friend!!! The sort of friend who'd keep their promises rather than the kind who'd break them and go to parties when they said they wouldn't!'

'You're mad!' shouts Jake. 'We wouldn't have gone to Suzie's if you hadn't cancelled your party!'

He turns around in a huff at the exact same moment that Suzie storms off from Alison . . .

The two of them collide into each other at full pelt. They both fall backwards, taking me, Alison and Keziah out in the process.

We all land in a huge heap on the muddy ground. Suzie ends up face-down in a puddle and starts screaming.

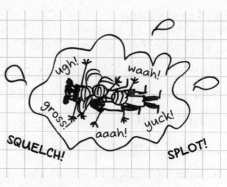

I've never met anyone so paranoid about dirt, germs or illness as Suzie Ashby. She always has a pack of wet wipes on her and is constantly washing her hands.

Washing your hands regularly is really important but Suzie takes it to a whole new level – she's been carrying antibacterial gel around with her ever since she was at playgroup.

Thank goodness for antibac gel – I need to wash my hands.

But you're in the bath! What a weirdo!

Before we can compose ourselves, a loud, deep voice booms across the playground . . . it's Mrs Edmonds.

'Right, you lot! No fighting in the playground! Detention for all of you!' she shouts, pointing at us. 'You, you, you, you, you AND you!'

'But it's nothing to do with me!' cries an innocent Axel who's been watching the whole thing bemused from under his tree.

'Do I look like I care?' she yells. 'Instead of free computer time at the end of the day, you will go straight to the school office and wait for me there. I will be calling your parents to let them know why you missed computing. You're all in BIG trouble.'

CHAPTER 6

Detention, Yay!

Detention?! None of us were

aware that our school even *gave out* detentions. I
have two older sisters who both came here and *they*
were never given one. This was obviously a Mrs
Edmonds thing, what with
her army background.

These children need
discipline, shame
they can't be court
marshalled, I'll
have to give them
detention, I guess!

We get told off or sent
to the green seats but
we never get detention.

I've been sent to the green seats once before
and it's NOT nice. You have to wait outside the
headteacher's office where everyone can see you
and stay there until you're called in. It could be
after two minutes or even two whole hours.

It's 3 a.m. — I've been waiting for thirteen hours!

Detention is a new one for me though, and worse still, free computer time is the one thing at school that EVERYONE looks forward to. Plus I suspect detention with Mrs Edmonds in charge is going to be horrific.

Right . . . before we get started, take an orange jumpsuit from the pile and I'm going to have to chain your ankles together!

I glance at Axel's watch – break will be over soon. Suzie runs off to the girls' toilets to clean herself up, armed with wet wipes and antibacterial gel from her rucksack. She's closely followed by Alison, apologising profusely as though the whole thing is all *her* fault. Meanwhile, Axel thinks the entire situation is hilarious. It's almost like he's relishing it and actually *looking forward* to detention.

Hanging out with friends? Wow! Detention is like having a social life!

'It'll be an adventure!' he grins. He makes eye contact with us too, which is kind of a breakthrough moment. An adventure?! We all look at him, confused.

That boy is seriously weird sometimes.

'Is she really gonna phone all our parents cos we slipped in the mud?' asks Keziah.

'She reckons we were fighting,' I reply.

'We're going to be in so much trouble,' Keziah sighs.

'My parents probably won't even care,' shrugs Jake, walking off towards the school building. 'They've got a lot on at the moment.'

I'm not sure what Jake means but I can't question it as he's already left. I suddenly have a horrible feeling that my parents might take my Aliana tickets away if they think I've been in trouble at school.

'Nooooooo, not my Altix . . .' I say, thinking out loud.

'Altix?!!' Keziah laughs.

'It's something Suzie came up with,' I say defensively. 'She said it first, not me!'

Ha ha! Hee hee!

I start laughing too.

'You really should give an *Altick* to Jake,' Keziah giggles. 'He loves Aliana's music and does the dance moves better than her!'

'I know,' I sigh. 'And in any other world they'd be his. But he's been acting so strange lately, I'm not sure he'd even want to go with me. Suzie seems to want it WAY more. She's been all over me. Jake's the complete opposite. He hasn't even mentioned the tickets since I got them. I should really let them have one each . . . I didn't even like Aliana till I got this birthday present.'

'Jake's got a lot on at the moment,' says Axel mysteriously from under his tree. We both turn to look at him, perplexed. That boy can be so strange. Axel, not Jake. Well, actually, both right now.

The bell rings, letting us know it's time to head back to class.

'You should definitely go to Suzie's, if only to see her house!' Keziah grins as we walk back in. 'Her bedroom looks massive on Instagram. I bet her place is huge. I can imagine her living in a mansion!'

ASHBY TOWERS

Sometimes talking to Keziah is just like talking to myself. We often think exactly the same thing at exactly the same time.

Suzie's not so bad after all!

Suzie's worse than I thought!

'Yeah!' I say excitedly. 'It's like you read my mind, Keziah! I want to have a good nosey! Suzie's the sort of person that would do lengths in her indoor heated swimming pool every morning or play tennis on her private court.'

'And she loves horse-riding,' adds Axel. 'Maybe there's a stable block!'

'And a paddock,' says Keziah.

By the time we're back in the classroom, we've decided Suzie lives in a stately home surrounded by acres of land, a helipad for quick helicopter trips away, a river with a mooring at the end of her garden and all manner of private staff, including Jeeves the butler who holds her chewing gum for her when she's finished chewing it.

My gum, Jeeves!

Oh yes, let me take that, miss, thank you. Can I keep it, please?

We chuckle away – we've almost forgotten about detention.

It pours with rain all afternoon. Ugh! Would Edmonds have us doing hundreds of press-ups out there? I don't think I could manage more than three. It would definitely be a physical form of detention rather than doing lines or essay writing.

No doubt she would have us performing army exercises, what with her military background.

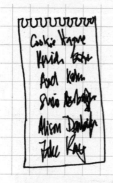

Besides, she took down our names on a piece of paper and I'm not being funny but handwriting is definitely NOT her strong point. I mean, she can barely write!

How on earth did she get a job as a teacher?

When the bell goes at the end of the day for free computing time, we all reluctantly trudge to meet Edmonds in the playground for our detention.

Luckily, the rain has turned to more of a mild drizzle now, so if she does make us do press-ups it won't be mid torrential downpour like the ones poor Martha Masters had to endure.

Edmonds hands us each a plastic bag, a pair of rubber gloves and a pair of tongs. Huh?! Tongs?!

'Right, children,' booms Edmonds. 'You are tasked with helping return the school nature garden to its former glory. The foxes have been here and there's rubbish everywhere. Don't forget to put your gloves on! Who knows, there might even be excrement out there!'

I explain to the others that excrement means poo. I've always liked long words. Nahid taught me this one when I pooed my pants once as a toddler.

'I knew what faeces meant but not excrement,' giggles Keziah. 'Faeces also means poo.'

Meanwhile, Suzie muffles a yelp, covering her

mouth with her hands so that Edmonds doesn't notice and make her do press-ups on the spot.

Because of that scream, you can do press-ups while picking up fox poo at the same time!

The foxes have been there alright. They've dragged some rubbish bags along from the bins and had a massive party by the look of things.

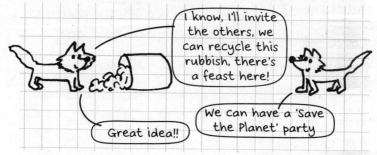

I know, I'll invite the others, we can recycle this rubbish, there's a feast here!

Great idea!!

We can have a 'Save the Planet' party

There's litter everywhere. The wildlife garden is wild at the best of times but right now it looks like a cross between a wasteland and a rubbish tip. We begin tonging up wrappers, newspaper, tissue, takeaway containers, all sorts . . .

'You, girl!' barks Mrs Edmonds, pointing at Suzie. 'Pick that up!'

Mrs Edmonds points to what looks like a massive fox poo.

Suzie starts wretching violently. We all try to

stifle our laughs so that Edmonds doesn't notice. Luckily, it's Axel to the rescue. Stealthy, like a ninja warrior, he swoops in, tongs up the poo (which actually turns out to be a rotten bit of baguette) and bags it. What a hero!

Don't worry. Super Axel has this covered!

(Rotten bit of baguette in a bag)

'Superb work,' says Edmonds when she notices the rotten bit of baguette has gone. She fails to notice that Suzie wasn't the one who got rid of it and is instead still recovering from her mini panic attack. Suzie is gasping and spluttering, while tears stream from her eyes.

When Edmonds' back is turned we all burst into hysterics – Suzie included. The rest of the detention passes quite quickly after that, with all of us working together diligently and actually getting along for once.

I really like Axel

Alison is OK after all

Keziah and Jake are OK after all

This lot are OK

Detention is really fun . . . hope I get more of these

Suzie even manages to conquer her fear and pick up a mouldy apple core.

She's really proud of herself and we all congratulate her. To be fair, it took some guts considering the state she was in moments earlier.

When we're finally back inside, it feels amazing to be safe, warm and dry again. Just as we're gathering up our stuff to go home for the day, Axel spots the school secretary, Mrs Jacoby, pinning something up on the noticeboard. We all crowd around.

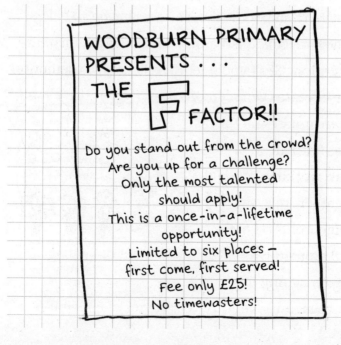

No way! Is a TV talent show coming to
Woodburn? Is this an after-school club to train us
up to be on it? What does the 'F' stand for? Fame?
Fortune? Fun? If this *is* an after-school club, twenty-

five pounds
is a bargain
for the whole
term. My
parents will
be delighted –
much cheaper
than childcare!

'OMG!' shrieks Suzie, 'This was meant to be!
I knew there was a reason we were all put in
detention. Can't you see? We're *meant* to do this. No
one else has even seen this poster yet as there's still

three minutes till the bell
goes for the end of
the day. Six places, and
there's . . . one, two, three,
four, five . . . *six* of us.'

Alison pulls a fluffy pink pen out of her bag and
begins signing us all up.

'What an adventure!' cries Axel, clapping his

hands and jumping up and down.

We're all really excited. Jake will blatantly win if this *is* a competition – his Aliana dance moves are amazing!

I'll look rubbish dancing next to him!

Me and Keziah could do some sort of double act. Mind you, Keziah gets horrific stage fright. That rules out singing and dancing . . . unless we're in some sort of disguise? Maybe a puppet show or something in full costume?

MEANWHILE ON STAGE LATER THAT MONTH . . .

Poor Keziah! Thank goodness I'm in the front of this horse – it would be awful to be at the back!

Poor Cookie! Thank goodness I'm at the back of this horse – it would be so embarrassing to be at the front!

Yay for detention! Now I just have to figure out where to get the twenty-five pounds from . . .

CHAPTER 7

Suzie's Mansion

When I get home after detention, I'm excited about the F Factor but worried about what Edmonds has said to my parents. What if they're fuming? What if they confiscate my Aliana tickets? I bet they're on the warpath. I needn't have worried though. Weirder than weird – they're being unusually nice to me!

Look, Abed! Our lovely daughter Cookie is home

Yes . . . she is lovely

Huh?

'We're so proud of you,' says Dad gleefully. 'The lovely new teacher Mrs Edmonds called to tell us that you were one of the six students picked for the special assignment at school today.'

Special assignment? Picking up fox poo? Well, bit of rotten baguette

'Well done, Cookie! Wonderful news!' says Mum. 'I've made you your favourite – chicken korma – to celebrate and there's chocolate cake for pudding.'

They're SO pleased with me. I'm not about to burst their bubble in a hurry.

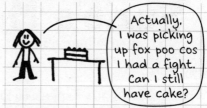

Actually, I was picking up fox poo cos I had a fight. Can I still have cake?

Edmonds has totally charmed my parents and even called me 'one of the smarter ones'. Crazy! She'd never actually met me before today, so how she's gathered all this info is beyond me.

I can tell just by looking at her . . . bright, high IQ, maybe a bit too temperamental though!

Definitely not an Aliana Tiny fan – I like her!

At least I'm not in trouble – that's one less thing to worry about – and they certainly aren't going to take away my gig tickets. Phew! I'm not even sure if Edmonds has told them what we were actually *doing* in detention – 'special assignment' seems way too grand a description. Mum and Dad are acting

like I'd been invited to
have lunch with the Prime
Minister, not picking up
soggy, rotten baguettes in
the rain. Special indeed!
I'm just going to leave
them to believe whatever
they want.

After a hot bath, I speak to Jake on the phone,
though not for very long as he's still being weird
with me. Then I speak to Keziah – for much longer
as she's not being weird at all. They've both had
exactly the same thing happen to them. Mrs
Edmonds is playing with our minds! Maybe this is
some sort of army tactic she's using to outsmart us.
Perhaps she's trying to freak us out or something?

I should really
thank her though,
as my parents are
super nice to me
for the rest of the
week. We have
pudding every

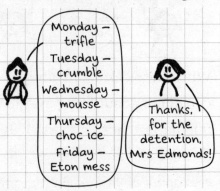

day, which is unheard of in our house!

Edmonds is also being super nice to us while continuing to be really mean to everyone else. It isn't a 'nice' kind of nice. It's the sort of nice where you're living in fear that if you make one false move that'll be it, 'nice' will turn into 'not-so-nice' and she'll come down on you like a ton of bricks.

It's the sort of 'nice' where you don't mind her making everyone else do a million press-ups in a rainstorm because you're so relieved it's not you. Scary nice!

School seems to put her on playground duty most days now, which is really taking the fun out of break time.

When the weekend finally comes around I'm in two minds about going over to Suzie's house. I keep fluctuating back and forth between quite looking forward to it and absolutely dreading it. I've hardly ever spent any time with her on my own, let alone on her home turf. It's kind of nerve-racking.

What would we talk about? We have NOTHING in common. My knowledge of Aliana Tiny, unicorns and pink things is pretty limited.

Yes . . . and their horns can come in handy for carrying doughnuts on . . .

What am I talking about?!

I could probably do press-ups for longer than I could talk to Suzie. The longest we've ever spent alone together is when we both came out of our toilet cubicles at the same time and washed our hands in neighbouring sinks. We

Awkward!

didn't say anything to each other then and now I'm going to her house for a WHOLE afternoon!

On Saturday morning I lie in bed thinking about how to get my hands on the twenty-five pounds for the F Factor.

I come up with three different options . . .

1. Ask my parents, but this runs the risk of them not wanting me to do it and scuppering the whole thing.

Mum, Dad, can I do the F Factor?

NO!!

2. Tell them it's an after-school club for people from the special assignment and it's such a privilege to have been chosen that I can't pass it up. Downside: I'd have to go somewhere else after school every week and kill time while they think I'm at the fake club.

3. See if I can return my bike voucher. I'll never be able to save up the rest of the money anyway!

The easiest and most hassle-free option right now is number three. I quickly get dressed and drag Roubi to the bike shop. We're already outside at 10 a.m. when it opens.

The sales assistant, Rod (according to his name-badge), is really grouchy and takes all of three seconds to inform me that they don't do refunds on gift vouchers.

Why didn't my parents give me actual money instead of a form of money limited to just one shop, so in fact worth less than real money?!

	£20 NOTE	£20 VOUCHER
COST	£20	£20
WHERE YOU CAN SPEND	Anywhere, accepted in all shops and outlets. ALL OF THEM	Only in Mike's Bikes. One shop in the WHOLE WORLD!

Maybe that's why they're throwing in the free bell? There are about three bells that cost under five pounds. I try to get one but grouchy Rod says that it can only be claimed when I redeem the voucher. Ugh! This voucher is a total con if you ask me! If I never save enough for a bike it's a complete waste of twenty-five pounds. I look around to see if there's anything else in the shop for the same price. I can just about afford a toddler's balance bike but apart from that it's all accessories, helmets, locks, lights and high-vis gear. All totally useless without an actual bicycle.

Wow, you look great! Got a new bike?

Nah — just the accessories. Bikes are overrated!

Waste of time. We walk home, bike-less.

That afternoon, Mum drops me off at Suzie's. It turns out she doesn't live in a mansion after all but her house is still pretty big. It has a driveway with an ornamental fountain in the middle of it and there are stone lions on each side of the front doorstep.

Suzie's mum, Janice, answers the door. Janice is bright orange with masses of swirly blonde hair and matching pink lips and nails. The two of them share all the same features – it's a bit like looking at Suzie from the future!

'You must be Cookie!' she says. 'Suzie's in the drawing room – I'll just get her.' She leaves me in the hallway alone with a massive golden mirror.

I look in it and feel VERY messy in this VERY tidy house. A drawing room? What even is a drawing room? A room for drawing in?!

'Sweetpea!' says Suzie, bounding over and throwing her arms around me.

She drags me off upstairs to her bedroom, which is just as massive and just as pink as it looks on Instagram. Plus, it has an en-suite bathroom! Jake may have a double bed but Suzie has her OWN BATHROOM. She introduces me to her Golden Retriever, Goldie, the family's Yorkshire Terrier, Yorkie, and her various other pets, including her budgie, Ziggy, which is short for Zig Zag.

'I came up with it myself,' she says proudly.

Next, she gives me a tour of her bedroom, including her wardrobe, dressing table and jewellery box . . .

The top drawer is rings, earrings in the bottom, necklaces and chains are in a secret compartment . . . Blah, blah, blah, zzzz . . .

. . . before showing me around the rest of the house. No swimming pool, no tennis court, no paddocks. BUT they do have a huge circular jacuzzi bathtub. Every room is immaculate: nothing is out of place. In the bedrooms all the bedding matches the curtains and throws. In the reception rooms, cushions, rugs and sofas are all colour-coordinated. In the kitchen, every surface is spotless and gleaming.

You could eat your dinner off me

Can't reach!

We fill the bathtub with loads of bubble bath and switch on the jets. Suzie's mum makes us milkshakes, which we sip as we sit on the edge soaking our feet in the masses of foam we've created.

This mango smoothie is great!

It's chocolate milkshake!

You must be smelling the bubble bath!

I needn't have worried about making conversation. Suzie just chats *at* me the whole time like she's eager to impress.

I really like animals and want world peace and think everyone should, and . . . blah . . . blah . . . blah!

It's as if she's on a first date and wants to make sure I ask her out again!

Plus, we keep doing activities the whole time so we don't really need to talk much. We play table football (I'm rubbish), sing karaoke (well, Suzie sings while I listen), make an assault course for her dog (who couldn't be less interested) and then she shows me the Aliana Tiny number she's hoping to perform for the F Factor (which is completely out of tune).

I'm quite relieved when her mum finally calls us down for dinner.

'Darling, it's your favourite,' she cries. 'Roast pork with crackling!'

Oh no! I've forgotten to tell them I don't eat pork and her mum's put on an enormous spread. The table is full of dishes: pigs in blankets (more pork), roast vegetables with bacon bits on top (more pork), and apple sauce (no pork as far as I'm aware). It's like I've been invited to a pork festival.

I have to think on my feet. 'Errr, I'm fasting,' I lie. 'It's Ramadan. But please, you guys tuck in.'

'But you drank a milkshake earlier?' says Suzie, confused.

Quite perceptive for her.

'Drinks don't count,' I lie. Again. Luckily, they seem to believe me and are blissfully unaware that Ramadan was actually in May, drinks *do* count and that my parents *never* let me fast anyway as they reckon I'm too young for it. Other kids at our school do it but I guess it's passed Suzie by. Phew. As I'm leaving Suzie's that evening she reminds me that there's an F Factor meeting on Monday. 'Dunno if I can do it,' I sigh. 'I still don't have the twenty-five pounds.'

'Mum!' yells Suzie. 'I need twenty-five pounds! NOW!'

'OK, darling,' comes the instant reply from the kitchen. Suzie grabs her mum's handbag off the hall table and fishes around in her purse before pulling out a couple of crisp banknotes – twenty-five pounds! She thrusts them into my hand.

'I can't accept this, Suzie,' I say. 'No way!'

'Well, how about I buy the other Aliana ticket off you?' she says, twisting her hair around her finger. 'We'll go together! It'll be amazeballs!'

I know I should really give the spare ticket to Jake as he would LOVE to go. But why should I? He's hardly even speaking to me! Suzie, on the other hand, has invited me round to her house. Besides, it's not like I'm just *giving* it to her, she's *buying* it off me. Plus, without it I risk missing out on the F Factor.

'OK,' I say finally. 'You can have the other ticket.' I reluctantly pull it out of my trouser pocket.

Suzie beams and hands me the twenty-five pounds.

She snatches the ticket off me a little bit too quickly and I have a sinking feeling in my stomach.

CHAPTER 8

Sniffling

Tickets for the Aliana gig are selling on the Internet for three hundred pounds and I've just sold one for twenty-five pounds. Am I mad?! I guess it's twenty-five pounds more than I'd get if I just gave it to Jake for free though, and at least now I won't miss out on the F Factor. It would be awful if the others ended up doing it without me. What if *they* all became best friends and *I* was left out of the group?!

Guys! Cookie's coming — quick, hide!

Club house

I wonder where everyone is?

Fear Of Missing Out

My FOMO is getting the better of me.

Poor Jake will be even more upset now.

He knows every single Aliana lyric and dance move. Maybe the gig ticket would have cheered him up? Am I a bad person?

I'm feeling a bit down at the moment

I'd love to cheer you up . . . but I can't think how!

Was Suzie only being nice to me yesterday so that I'd give her the ticket? Maybe now that she's got what she wanted, she'll go back to being her mean old self again?

Got the ticket! Now I can be mean to Cookie again!

COOKIE – YOU SUCK!! MWAH HA HA HA!

Ugh! If I'd sold the ticket for three hundred pounds on the Internet I could have bought a bike from Mike's Bikes by now. I could have bought three bikes! I saw one I quite liked for a hundred pounds when I was in there on Saturday. I sigh and put the twenty-five pounds away in an envelope ready to hand in to the school office before the F Factor meeting.

I can't wait to find out more details about it all.

The whole thing has been a bit vague and mysterious so far. After we signed up last week, the six of us found notes in our bags stating the following . . .

Dear Cookie Haque

Congratulations on being selected for the F Factor. The first session will be this coming Monday in the school gym from 3.25–4.05 p.m. Please pay the £25 joining fee in a clearly marked envelope to the school office before then in order to secure your place.

* THANK YOU *

There was no signature, no contact details, no more information. Odd.

The following Monday, I'm wondering what the F Factor has in store when Axel shouts out to me from under his tree. 'Hey Cookie! I wanna show you something. I already showed Keziah last week and she liked it.' He's all excited, and adds, 'It's even better now cos I've been practising all weekend. It's a secret though, OK?'

'Uh, OK, sure,' I reply. I've no idea what on earth he's talking about. Masked by the tree so no one but me can see, he drops his bag down and crouches with his hands on the floor. The next bit is kind of bizarre. He puts his feet over his shoulders and walks forward on his hands, balancing precariously for about five seconds before toppling over.

'Do you like it?' he asks.

'Err, yeah,' I say. I'm not quite sure if I do like it. If he'd have kept it up for longer it might have looked impressive.

'Gonna put it to music and add a few jumps at the beginning and do it for the F Factor,' he says proudly.

'Great!' I reply sceptically as we head inside.

By lunchtime, I'm starving. I was worrying about Jake and the ticket so much this morning that I didn't have any appetite for breakfast. I go to the school office and hand in my twenty-five pounds,

clearly marked
with my name
and 'F FACTOR

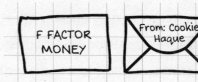

MONEY' in capitals on the envelope.

'I didn't think that would be your kind of
thing, Cookie,' says Mr Hastings, the deputy head,
glancing over from the photocopier. 'Good on you!'

'Thanks?' I reply, a little confused.

Mr Hastings is a bit of a Jekyll-and-Hyde
character. Nice as pie on a good day but on a bad
day he turns really mean and short-tempered. It's

like someone
else's personality
has been
transplanted
into his body.

Thankfully today is a good day. He winks at me
in a friendly manner and walks off.

Why *wouldn't* it be my thing? What *is* my thing?
Being boring and doing homework? Being square
and unglamorous? Well, Mr Hastings . . . I've got
news for you! I AM glamorous! I'm going to the
Aliana Tiny gig with Suzie Ashby and the F Factor
IS my thing. SO. THERE. As though she'd heard

97

me mention Suzie even though I'd only thought it in my head, Alison Denbigh enters the office at that exact moment to hand over her twenty-five pounds. Now *she* is being overly nice to me too. Oh boy! Don't tell me she's after my other ticket. Maybe I should let her have it . . . for three hundred pounds! Bikes all round, Jake and Keziah!

'So exciting about the F Factor!' says Alison. 'We'll all have such fun together. Did you have a good time with Suzie on Saturday?' she adds casually. 'What did you do?'

'Not much,' I reply.

'Did you have milkshakes?' she asks more urgently. 'Did you put your feet in the jacuzzi?! Did her mum make you a buffet?'

I think she's trying to work out whether we had more fun together than Suzie has with her or something like that. Bit FOMO if you ask me!

'Love to stay and chat, Ali-pie, but gotta run!

Catch you later!' I call out over my shoulder as I race off to the canteen. The last thing I want is to get caught up in a bizarre love triangle with Alison Denbigh and Suzie Ashby.

By the time I reach the canteen, I'm starving. It smells like heaven. The Thai chicken curry option looks AMAZING. I think I'll get Selina to dish me out an extra ladlefull. Just as I get to the front of the queue, a voice calls out to me.

'Babes! Don't forget you're fasting for Hanukkah!'

It's Suzie. Great . . . I'd forgotten about the pork festival lie.

Me: 'Ramadan actually, and yeah, I was, errr . . . just queuing to say hi to Selina.'

Suzie: 'Who?'

Me: 'Errr, my favourite dinner lady.'

Suzie: 'What?! Bit weird . . . '

Me: 'And, err . . . to get a drink as well.'

Suzie: 'OK, well, come find me! We have lots to discuss . . . like what to wear to the Aliana concert. I'm thinking my pink unicorn jumpsuit. I'll save you a seat, hun!'

And with that, she flounces off. I look over at Jake and Keziah, who I usually sit with at lunch. They're deep in conversation. What are they chatting about? They look so intense. Is Jake being mean about me to Keziah? Or maybe I'm just having another bout of FOMO?

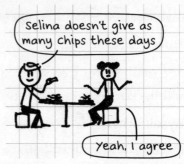

'What ya having, Cookie?' asks Selina when I get to the front of the lunch queue. 'Thai chicken curry is my top tip. Double helping for my fave gal?'

'Oh, no, I'm not hungry, thanks!' I reply through gritted teeth as Susie smiles at me across the lunch hall. 'Just wanted to say hi!'

'Well, hi there, young lady,' says Selina, baffled, as my stomach growls furiously, begging me to reconsider.

I pour myself a glass of water and wonder who I'll end up sitting next to. Jake and Keziah or Suzie . . .

Suzie is sitting alone whereas Jake and Keziah have each other. If I join them I might be interrupting their little party – they look as thick as thieves. Maybe they're discussing what fun the

'Save the Planet' party was *without* me. I walk over to Suzie and plonk myself down next to her and watch her eat as I sip on my water and starve to death.

Surrounded by the sight of Thai chicken curry, baked potatoes and ratatouille, on top of the sound of clinking knives and forks, I'm ravenous. It's unbearable!

'Budge up, guys,' says Alison, trying to join us.

'There's not enough room!' says Suzie. 'Besides, Cookie and I are trying to have lunch together. We have Aliana business to discuss.'

'It's OK,' I say, trying to make my escape. 'I'm not even eating.'

'Don't be silly,' says Suzie, grabbing my hand and pulling me back down.

'Fine,' says Alison, walking off to sit on her own.

When lunch is finally over and everyone is playing outside, I leg it back to the canteen to find Selina. I tell her I'm starving and don't know what came over me earlier when I skipped lunch. She doesn't even question it! Instead, she immediately sorts me out with a massive baked potato and cheese to go, which I take to the cloakroom and wolf down in a frenzy.

Steady on! I'll get indigestion!

At last, food!

Food, glorious food! Bliss! I lean back in between everyone's jackets and bags, relieved that I've finally managed to eat something. All of a sudden I hear sniffling and realise that someone is crying. I duck down, hiding behind a bunch of coats, and sneak a tiny peak. There, coming out of the girls' toilets and sobbing into a wad of loo roll, red-eyed and miserable, is Alison Denbigh.

Poor Alison! I can't help but feel this is all my fault.

CHAPTER 9

The F Factor

In class that afternoon, Alison is acting like the crying episode never happened. She's trying really hard to impress Suzie and is being all smiley and giggly, and constantly whispering stuff to her. I say 'trying' because Suzie isn't giving much back. Alison keeps persevering though. Did I imagine the whole crying thing? Is my brain playing tricks on me due to a lack of food? I definitely saw her crying. I know I did. Plus, on closer inspection her eyes do look a bit red and puffy.

I'm having fun, honest I am!

I feel sorry for Alison. Imagine being so on edge about your friendship and constantly having to put on a show for Suzie the whole time. It must be utterly exhausting. Suzie is so high maintenance. Maybe I should just let Jake go to the Aliana gig instead of me. It would probably be a really stressful evening with Suzie there anyway and he's much more laid-back than I am.

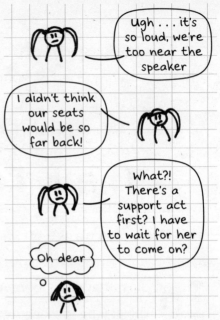

No one in class is paying much attention to the lesson. There's loads of hushed chattering and murmuring going on. Mrs Mannan is getting really annoyed but can't do much about it as she's struggling to work her new electronic whiteboard.

It keeps crashing whenever she tries to write on it. 'Turn it off then on

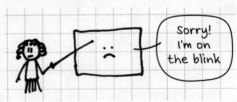

again,' says Jake, trying to be helpful. 'That often does the trick.'

Mrs Mannan clearly doesn't appreciate his offer of technological expertise.

'I know what to do, thank you very much, Jake Kay,' she snaps. 'If I need your help, I'll ask for it.'

'Sorry I even spoke,' mumbles Jake.

'Good!' she replies sternly. 'Because as you know, Jake, talking out of turn in class is against school policy.'

SCHOOL POLICY
- Turn up
- Wear uniform
- Be good
- Whatever else Mrs Mannan decides

She looks back at the whiteboard, flustered, then turns it off and on again to try and reboot it.

Having never ever mentioned the Aliana tickets before, out of the blue Jake casually brings them up.

'So, what are you gonna do with your Aliana tickets? Any ideas?'

This is awkward. He obviously wants them.

'I, errr . . . need to see . . . Roubi might want to go with me,' I blurt out, trying to think on my feet. I hate lying to Jake – it feels awful. Here I am judging Suzie on how she treats Alison and meanwhile I'm acting no better myself. The shame!

'*Roubi*?!' he says, surprised. 'I wouldn't have thought Aliana would be her thing.'

Aliana?! Are you serious?! I think I'm going to be sick! . . . and it's on the same day as a by-election!

'She goes through all sorts of strange phases,' I lie.

More lying. I hate it. I try to convince myself I'm lying to protect Jake's feelings, that I'm a nice person really. But my FOMO means I can't quite bring myself to give up the ticket.

'No worries', says Jake understandingly. 'Roubi *is* your sister. Of course you have to give it to her!' This makes me feel even worse.

'Hush, Jake, please!!!' snaps Mrs Mannan. 'I'm trying to concentrate! I'm convinced this thing has gremlins in it,' she adds, angrily pressing buttons on the whiteboard control and furiously leafing through the user manual.

'Gremlins?!' repeats Alison, turning pale.

'Yeah, means it's haunted,' says Suzie, trying to wind Alison up, which is pretty easy to do as she's really gullible – she'll believe just about anything!

'My mum told me this whole school is haunted,' says Finlay Riordan. 'It was built in Victorian times when there were loads of ghosts around. Once she even went to see a psychic called Mystical Marjorie who told her that she would soon have a minor injury. Three weeks later, she tripped up in the playground and cut her chin.'

Everyone gasps.

'What's a psychic?' asks Alison.

'Someone who can talk to ghosts,' replies Suzie matter-of-factly.

Alison lets out a loud yelp, all remaining colour draining from her face. Jake rolls his eyes. 'I can't believe anybody still believes in ghosts in this day and age. And pleeaaasssse don't get me started on psychics.'

'I know, right?' I agree. 'There's no science behind them whatsoever. Such a waste of time and money.'

'Total con!' he nods. We laugh.

'Talking of ghosts,' I say, 'Alison looks like one right now.'

We both glance over at her. She's wide-eyed and white as a sheet. We laugh some more – probably a bit too loudly.

'STOP!!!!' screams Mrs Mannan, clearly at the end of her tether. Alison falls off her chair, terrified that the screaming has come from the haunted whiteboard.

'All this talking ends NOW!' snaps Mrs Mannan. She then proceeds to separate me and Jake. Suzie instantly shoots her hand up in the air and offers

to swap places with him so SHE can sit next to ME!
Uh oh . . . she'll probably just want to talk about
unicorns and the Aliana gig the whole time. This
could be FULL-ON.

After school finishes for the day, the six of us
F-Factorers make our way to the gym hall for our
first meeting. We're all really excited.

'Isn't karate club usually in the hall after school
today?' asks Alison.

'Yeah, that's a good point. But we need to use the
stage for our acts so we have to be in here,' declares
Suzie.

'Hang on!' says
Alison. 'We're no way
near stage-ready.'

'I am,' replies Suzie.

'Seriously?' I say.
'Me and Keziah don't
even know what we're
doing for our act yet.'

'You're doing an act *together*?' says Suzie, as though she's actually jealous. 'It's just . . . I thought maybe you and I would do something together, Cookie, babes?'

'Huh?' says Alison, looking distraught for about the millionth time today.

'Thought you were stage-ready?' says Jake. 'Hardly stage-ready if you don't even know whether you're in an act with Cookie or not.'

'Just an alternative option,' says Suzie, shrugging. 'No matter. I'm better off solo anyway.'

Can't reach . . .
Maybe I should've
been with Alison,
this isn't going
to work

'Or *we* could do something together, Suzie?' Alison offers.

Suzie just laughs this off. Poor Alison. This really isn't her day.

The back half of the hall is full of karate clubbers warming up on mats. We sit on some benches at

the front near the stage, as none other than Mrs
Edmonds enters the room.

'Is *she* taking
karate club these
days?' I ask. 'Poor
karate clubbers.
That must be
ZERO fun.'

'Bet they're wishing they'd never signed up,'
laughs Keziah.

'Bet she's a black belt,' says Axel.

She probably is a black belt – not only in karate
but in every martial art going.

But instead of
heading towards
the karate clubbers,
Edmonds walks
right past them and
straight over to us.
Great. Here goes.
She's gonna tell us
off for loitering
after school
or something.

Well, we aren't loitering, Mrs Edmonds. We are F-Factorers! So you can take your one thousand press-ups AND your detention and give them to someone else, thank you very much!

'Right then, you lot,' she booms. 'Let's get to it!'

She winks at us all. Get to what?

Huh?! What on earth is going on? More mind games? We look at each other, nervous and confused. Are we about to be punished? She hasn't even accused us of loitering yet.

Edmonds clears her throat with a deep cough, and says, 'Welcome to the F Factor!'

What?! Why would Mrs Edmonds be taking us for the F Factor? Was the drama teacher off sick? In what way is Mrs Edmonds even qualified to do something like this?

Maybe she entertained the troops in a warzone?

And for my next trick I'll be fire eating!

'Looks like our F Factor gang are one and the same as last Monday's detention group!' she says. 'All my favourite students! What fun!'

Favourite students?! You don't even know us! You've only met us once. And we hardly spoke! We just picked up rubbish!

She then turns to Alison and says, 'As for you, you look like someone's just decapitated your favourite teddy bear. Come on, cheer up!'

Alison attempts a weak smile but it's convincing no one. Poor Alison. Again.

I'm having a terrible day!

Edmonds then goes on to tell us about The *Forest* Factor. Yep, you heard me. Forest! Not fame. Not fortune. Not fun. And not any other good F words either. Just forest.

F WORDS
Fear
Fabulous
Funny
Fantastic
~~Fantasmagorical~~ *

Ugh! I could have put that twenty-five pounds towards my

* Phantasmagorical begins with ph . . . (it means crazy, surreal and fantastic)

new bike. I'll never afford it now. So tragic! Instead, I'll be doing 'fun' things in the great outdoors like picking up rotten, mouldy baguettes, no doubt.

We've basically all just paid twenty-five pounds to be in detention every week for the whole term!!!! Unbelievable!!!

Suzie and Alison make out that they knew the F Factor was Forest Club all along.

Suzie always has to save face in life and can never front up to getting anything wrong. This time it's much to Alison's delight as it gives them something to bond over.

Axel is also thrilled but, then again, he was thrilled to be in *actual* detention so this comes as no great surprise. Plus, apparently, he loves forests! He and Keziah even high-five each other! I think she's a bit relieved. For Keziah, anything is better than performing on a stage or being in a talent show, even if it involves picking up rotten old baguettes off the floor. There's no worry of drying up on with Forest Club, I guess.

I lean over and whisper to Jake, 'Are we actually gonna stick with this thing?'

'Well, we've paid for it,' he shrugs, 'and it keeps us out the house.'

Jake never seems to want to go home these days. So odd.

He's right though. We have paid, so we may as well get our money's worth. Maybe it will be fun? We actually ended up having a laugh picking up rubbish. My inner FOMO is telling me that I don't want to miss out on anything. Whatever that 'anything' might be . . .

CHAPTER 10

Forest Club

The rest of the meeting is taken up with 'housekeeping announcements'. In other words, admin and rules. Boring! This includes what clothing is suitable for Forest Club, how bad behaviour won't be tolerated at Forest Club and what we can all expect to be doing at Forest Club. We're also told that if we really earn it, there will be an extra-special something for us all to look forward to. Woo hoo!!! Let me guess . . . a 'Picking Up Fox Poo' party!

Three cheers for fox poo!

At least if there *is* a party, it'll be an eco-friendly one. Forest Club is about all things nature and all things environment. We are way more likely to save the planet here than at any 'Save the Planet' party of Suzie's.

Mrs Edmonds passes some handouts around: a list of appropriate outdoor-wear like waterproofs and wellington boots; a list of handy accessories like compasses and torches; and finally a reading list, including books like *The Outdoor Survival Handbook* and *The Secret Life of Trees*. She says this is in case we fancy some extra bedtime reading. Errr . . . let me think about that . . . *The Secret Life of Trees*? No, thanks!

'Torch?' says Keziah, reading off the list of essentials. 'Are we gonna be in the dark?'

'If it gets dark,' says Edmonds bluntly.

Keziah looks a tad freaked out.

'Will there be ghosts?' asks Alison.

'There might be . . .' replies Mrs Edmonds, 'if such a thing as ghosts exist.'

Now Alison looks freaked out too. F Factor?

More like Freak-Out Factor!

Alison tells us afterwards that next month her parents are taking the whole family on a weekend away to her great-aunt's mansion. It's a big deal as lots of her relatives are flying in from abroad. Her great-aunt lives in an amazing old stately home in the countryside, but Alison has read on the Internet that it's rumoured the lady of the house from Georgian times still roams the corridors at night.

No need to be scared, Alison, I'm your great-great-great-great-great-great-aunt!

Ever since then she's been in a right state. She says that most nights she doesn't sleep at all for worrying about ghosts.

Poor Alison. I guess that explains why she's so jumpy and fragile at the moment.

Ugh! Go away, ghosts . . . I just want to count sheep again like in the good old days!

This club is certainly not doing anything to relieve our fears. If we end up climbing trees, which we might well do considering trees are what you get in forests, then Axel will be terrified too, what with his fear of heights. If we're outdoors the whole time, I'm sure there'll be lots of droppings and poo about the place, not to mention other germs and bacteria to freak Suzie out. And my FOMO has already struck, otherwise I would have left Forest Club by now! That only leaves Jake 'I'm not scared of anything' Kay. If he was scared of forests then we'd have a full house on the fear bingo checklist!

'Sorry, miss,' Jake pipes up bravely, 'but I've got to ask . . . what's all this F Factor stuff got to do with being *talented*?'

None of us had dared to question the fact that the advert for the F Factor we'd seen on the noticeboard had been more than a little misleading. Well, not until now, that is. We'd all kept quiet, fearing the wrath of Edmonds.

Uh oh! What have you done, Jake? Edmonds obviously wanted to trick us into joining her weird Forest Club. No one would have signed up if the poster had told the truth . . .

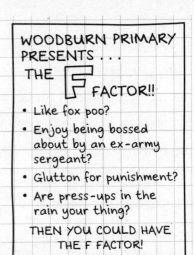

Does he seriously want us to get some horrific punishment because of *him* and *his* braveness?! We've all been keeping our mouths shut for a reason. Edmonds clears her throat. Uh oh . . . we're in for it now . . .

'Very good, Kay. Very perceptive,' she barks, delighted. 'You will need to be talented because forest school is all about survival. Survival of the forest! Survival of the fittest!'

Forest *school*? I thought this was a *club*?! *Survival*?!

We're not in a war zone!!
Survival of the *fittest?!*
Well, that rules me out.

You're not in the army now, Edmonds, although she clearly still thinks she is. All this barking at people and calling them by their surnames, not to mention her love of punishment!

As we leave the meeting, Axel looks like he's about to burst with excitement. What a weirdo. The rest of us, on the other hand, are a bit more unsure.

The week flies by and before we know it, we find ourselves at our first official Forest Club meeting. We all gather in the playground. Axel has drawn war stripes on his cheeks with face paint and is wearing a head band.

Suzie and Alison are in matching combat outfits complete with camouflage scrunchies tying their hair back.

Even Keziah and Jake look
ready for an adventure, dressed
in khakis and army greens.

I feel a bit scruffy in comparison,
looking down at my battered old stripy
anorak and bobbly jogging bottoms.

'You!' orders Edmonds. 'Pick a partner. For
our first exercise,
Foresters, everyone
will be in pairs.'

Poor girl is from a
family of tramps. I'll
let her have first
pick of a partner

Oh boy! Who should I choose? This is an unusual
situation for me. I'm used to being picked way
past the halfway point in PE team picking (I'm not
very sporty), but getting to do the actual choosing
– *this* is new to me. Suddenly Jake, Keziah, Suzie,
Alison and Axel are all staring at me like they're
puppies in a pet shop, each of them desperate to be

chosen. Suzie is looking
particularly eager. Who
should it be? With great
power comes great
responsibility . . . help!!!!

Ip, dip, sky
blue . . . Huh?
What does
that even
mean?

Usually I'd pick Keziah as she's my best friend
but Jake is a close second and I feel bad that I lied to

him about my gig tickets. It's like I owe him now. But if I don't pick Suzie, the gig will be unbearable. In fact, my life will be unbearable.

Am I turning into Alison? Just doing everything to please Suzie?

COOKIE OOKIE OOKION ALISON

It's because of her I starved at lunchtime the other day. Being friends with Suzie . . . what kind of a life is this?!

'Come on, Haque!' booms Edmonds. 'We don't have all year.'

I'm dying!

Hooray, we're best friends!

I need to decide quickly! Arghhhh . . . hang on though! If it wasn't for Suzie I couldn't even have done Forest Club. She gave me the twenty-five pounds! Jake and Keziah didn't even give me a birthday present!! They just went to Suzie's party WITHOUT ME!!! Mind you, I did give Suzie the Aliana ticket that should really have gone to Jake. Then again, she's still being really nice to me even after she got the ticket. She must be genuine. She does actually like me . . .

'Hurry up, Haque!!' barks Edmonds so loudly that I pretty much jump in the air, and impulsively blurt out, 'Suzie!' before I've actually managed to finish thinking it through. Ugh! I've been forced into a knee-jerk reaction. I can't make eye contact with Jake or Keziah now. Keziah will be OK – she's pretty cool about most things – but wait till Jake finds out that me and Suzie are going to see Aliana at

Wembley together. It doesn't bear thinking about. I push the thought to the back of my head.

'That took you long enough,' says Suzie, beaming that I've chosen her. Meanwhile, Alison looks as though she's been slapped in the face.

'Errr, yeah. I was miles away,' I lie. 'I was thinking about what I want for dinner.' More lying. It's becoming a way of life.

COOKIE HAQUE
(Business Card)

- Professional liar
- No lie too small!

CH LIES LTD P.T.O. for contact details

'No eating till sundown though, Cookie!' says Suzie. 'You're still fasting, right?'

'Yeah, right,' I reply. I've been avoiding eating in front of Suzie for over a week now and the whole thing is starting to turn into a total joke. Waiting till she leaves the canteen, sitting down low, hiding out of sight, snacking secretly. It's like something out of a comedy show and no one knows apart from Selina, who is helping me out with my deception!

Here, quick – shove these Cornish pasties down your top!

Suzie doesn't even seemed to have noticed that I'm the only person in the whole school observing Ramadan this year.

I'm very religious – I fast when I don't need to . . .

Good girl!

Edmonds takes us to the wooded area round the back of the school. Our first challenge is to make minibeast hotels using natural materials. They're a place for bugs and little beasties to thrive, breed and shelter.

MINIBEAST HOTEL

125

This might actually be fun . . .

Hmm . . .

We could go to town and make it a hotel complex! We could use dead wood for creepy crawlies and put out leaves for ladybirds as they eat aphids, which hang out on leaves. Hmm, if we put it near some nectar-rich flowers we'd attract birds and butterflies and bees. Maybe we could make a larger section from stone for frogs and toads in winter so they could avoid the frost as it would create the cool, damp conditions that they like. If we're feeling wild we could even make a hedgehog box at the bottom!! This is so exciting!!!

'Ewwww! Gross!' screeches Suzie. 'We'll get our nails dirty! We may as well just empty the contents of the school bins like the foxes did – ready-made minibeast hotel complete with bacteria, germs and disgusting little creatures! Yuck!'

Oi, how rude! That's my home you're talking about!

Suzie does not share my enthusiasm for this activity. I look over at Keziah who's partnered with Jake. They're having a great old time. Even Alison and Axel seem to be having fun together.

'Surely you're not into the idea?!' asks Suzie.

'Err . . . nah, not really . . .' I lie for a quiet life, although I'm secretly annoyed. Yet more lies. I can't

Maybe as well as beetles, bugs, worms, ants and slugs, we may attract some mini unicorns!

Uh oh, I'm lying again!

be bothered to convince her this would be fun. Too much effort.

K&J'S BEDBUGS & BREAKFAST

← Keziah + Jake's

At the end of the session, Keziah and Jake have made 'K and J's Bedbugs and Breakfast' complete with the cutest mini wooden sign EVER.

Axel and Alison have made nothing short of a minibeast skyscraper with about ten separate levels – a feat of insect engineering and a very impressive design, given they only used bits of old wood, pine cones and the like.

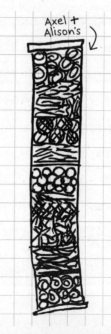

Axel + Alison's

127

← Ours
(just a pile
of old twigs)

Ugh, I'm out
of here!

Hotel? More of a
shack . . . I'll give it
a zero-star review
on TripAdvisor

Meanwhile, me and Suzie have very little to show for ourselves. I can see Edmonds is disappointed and to be honest so am I.

Why didn't I stand up to Suzie? Why didn't I pick someone else in the first place? Why am I pushing my two best friends away? What's more, I'm beginning to quite like Edmonds and I'm sad I've let her down. That evening I feel miserable. I go to bed without eating anything, and it's not even Ramadan . . .

CHAPTER 11

Scavenger Hunt!

How can I get out of being partnered with Suzie at Forest Club? I mean, why even bother with it if you're worried about getting dirt under your nails?! Everyone else seems really into the whole thing now. Plus, we're all starting to like Mrs Edmonds – she always has our back at break times these days. We're her gang.

We can be a little more unruly than the other kids and get away with it. If we drop a tissue we can just pick it up without having to do a gazillion press-ups like poor Martha Masters. We have an understanding.

Axel! You've dropped some crisp packets, chocolate wrappers and sweet papers! NEVER MIND ... happens to the best of us!

Having to pretend I'm not eating at lunchtimes means that I'm not hanging out with Keziah and Jake as much as I want to. Any time I've tried to declare that fasting is finally over, I've chickened out. What am I scared of? Suzie?!

Meanwhile, I'm really missing Jake. At one point I was practically living round his house. I haven't been over there in ages now. I usually walk home from school with him but these days he ALWAYS has an excuse not to, like he urgently needs to pick something up for his mum from the shops or return an overdue library book. It's like he's trying to avoid me. When I need my fix of Keziah, we can just speak on the phone. Jake, on the other hand, is never home to chat. In school, he seems distant all of the time . . . miles away, deep in thought.

Is it because I haven't offered him an Aliana ticket yet? The subject will come up again sooner or later. Keziah keeps telling me I should get over my FOMO and let him go to the gig with Suz...

It would make him so happy. He wouldn't even mind if he had to go with Edmonds! Now *that* I would like to see ... Mrs Edmonds at an Aliana gig!

I'm so desperate to get out of Forest Club before next week's session that I even consider inventing

violin lessons that I can pretend to go to instead. But I'd never get away with it ...

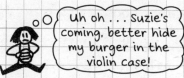

Besides, I don't want to do any more lying right now.

The fact that I spent twenty-five pounds (or rather, an Aliana ticket) to be able to go to Forest Club means that I have to see it through. Plus, if I did quit, Jake and Keziah would still keep going without me. It would be like Suzie's party all over again. Who knows? They might even end up moving in next door to each other and sharing a cat! Ugh! My

getting the better of me. How has this ...ened?! An Altick worth three hundred ... on the black market in exchange for Forest Cl... with Suzie as my partner?!!

HOW IT ALL HAPPENED . . .

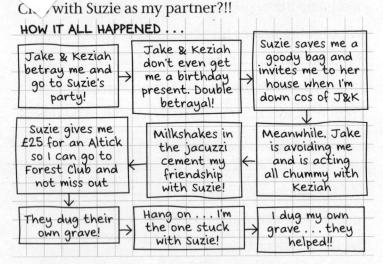

| Jake & Keziah betray me and go to Suzie's party! | → | Jake & Keziah don't even get me a birthday present. Double betrayal! | → | Suzie saves me a goody bag and invites me to her house when I'm down cos of J&K |

Meanwhile, Jake is avoiding me and is acting all chummy with Keziah

Milkshakes in the jacuzzi cement my friendship with Suzie!

Suzie gives me £25 for an Altick so I can go to Forest Club and not miss out

They dug their own grave!

Hang on . . . I'm the one stuck with Suzie!

I dug my own grave . . . they helped!!

Maybe there's a way I can switch partners to be with Keziah or Jake at the next session? I'd happily partner with Axel too. I wonder whether on some level Alison prefers being with Axel. Despite the fact that she wouldn't ordinarily want to be paired with someone who she thinks is unpopular, they seemed to have so much fun making their minibeast skyscraper together. She must know deep down that she could never have had *that* much fun with Suzie.

This minibeast skyscraper is FAB!

And so is our whole planet!

But it's full of germs

I needn't have been dreading our second session though, because the next Forest Club meeting is AMAZING! I haven't had so much fun in ages!

The first thing Edmonds says is, 'OK, Foresters! We're going to split into two teams of three today. Who wants to be a team leader?' Everyone shoots their hands into the air and Keziah and Alison get chosen. They take it in turns to pick team members.

I needn't worry about being picked last, as Keziah will definitely pick me first – which she does (making me feel awful for picking Suzie as my partner last week). Alison then chooses Suzie (also predictable), Keziah chooses Jake and lastly Axel ends up on Suzie's team. Axel is used to being picked last and doesn't seem that fussed about it.

Just as I thought, Alison does seem pleased about getting Axel on her team. She was probably just too

scared to choose him first because of Suzie!!

'Today's activity is an A to Z scavenger hunt,' booms Mrs Edmonds. 'Armed with these printouts and checklists, you must try to find an item from the woods for each letter of the alphabet. Don't expect to get all twenty-six – you're not miracle-workers. However, I will tell you that some items have been specially hidden for you to make your quest a little easier. OK, teams! Take up your arms and good luck!'

Take up your arms? We aren't going into battle!

I just know this is going to be fun. Maybe it will be like a battle . . . I can imagine Axel getting quite competitive over this. Although with Suzie 'I don't want to get my hands dirty' Ashby on his team, perhaps not.

Mrs Edmonds has printed out loads of pointers and clues for us. There are specimen jars, as well as the checklists to help us collect and identify stuff. Axel's right – Forest Club *is* an adventure!

Jake is being much quieter than usual. I'm trying to work out whether it's just with me or if he's being weird with Keziah too. It's hard to tell as we're all over the shop trying to 'scavenge' things against the clock! He keeps giving me one-word answers to everything . . .

He's also refusing to make eye contact with me when he speaks. Even Axel manages to look at the ground less often than this! What

on earth is going on with him? Is he annoyed that I picked Suzie as my partner last week? Or maybe that Keziah picked me over him, despite the fact that I picked Suzie over both of them the other day?

Keziah never holds grudges. She thinks it's funny that I chose Suzie by accident and then hated Forest Club as a result! I have no idea what is up with Jake . . .

Still, the clock is ticking and we have some serious scavenging to do. We venture deeper into the wooded area, which is very shaded as the trees are densely packed together.

'Has anyone got their torch handy?' asks Keziah. 'It's pretty dark in here.'

'I have,' says Jake, 'but come on! You can tough it out, Keziah. You don't need a torch!'

Hmmm, well, she definitely *is* getting more than one-word answers from him. Maybe he's just being off with *me*?

If I'm extra nice to Keziah that'll show Cookie!

'Ah, come on, Jake. Pretty please!' pleads Keziah.

'Yeah, how would you like it if you were scared of something?' I say, joining in to support her. 'Which obviously you're *not* because *nothing* scares you, right?!'

'Not this again!' he says, loosening up a bit. 'I told you! I honestly can't think of anything that scares me!'

'How about this spider?!'
I say, picking up a spider and
dangling it in front of his nose.

Oi – put me down! Don't involve me in your arguments!

'Nope!' he says proudly,
finally making eye contact with me. . . progress!

'I know what your fear is,' says Keziah. 'That
Cookie will never stop asking you what your fear is!'

'That's it!' He grins. 'You got me!'

We all laugh. 'By the way that's a daddy-long-legs,
not a spider – they
have much longer
legs and smaller
bodies.'

Having a big body and little legs would be so weird . . .

'OK, thanks for
that, wise guy!' I reply. 'Fear of daddy-long-legses
doesn't quite have the same ring as arachnophobia!'
We laugh some more. Jake puts the daddy-long-legs
in a little jar and we write it down on our list for the
letter D. Jake seems to have come out of his shell at
last. Phew! We're
doing pretty well
and are whizzing
through the
alphabet.

Wow, guys! We're whizzing through the alphabet!

How many letters in the alphabet, again?!

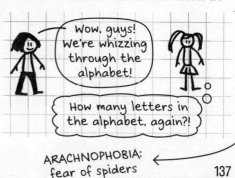

ARACHNOPHOBIA:
fear of spiders

137

We're on a roll rushing about looking for things, collecting things and identifying things, all the while teasing the other team that we're doing better than them. The others also seem to be having fun, although Suzie appears to be doing less of the fieldwork and more of the bossing around while waving her clipboard about!

This is the opposite of last week's Forest Club. Running around the woods with my friends is such fun. I feel so happy and free. All six of us are having the time of our lives. Jake is back to being my buddy again. This is GREAT. SO GREAT. Unfortunately, it doesn't last . . .

CHAPTER 12

A - ZZZZZZZZZ

We zip through the first half of the alphabet in no time at all.

A Ant – we find about a million of these under a bit of bark that we pull off a fallen, withered tree. There are so many of the little critters that we decide to use them for I and Q as well – see later!*

> Wow! I usually get picked last

B Bark – the one and the same bit we found all the ants under!

> Woof woof! (Just kidding!)

C Conker – I happen to have some in my pocket already because someone once told me that they're good for getting rid of spiders. I found two in my bedroom the other day (spiders, not conkers, that is). Strictly speaking this is cheating as I actually put them in my pocket last week when I found them on the way home from school (conkers, not spiders, that is). But, hey – we're up against the clock so it's all in the name of time-saving!!!

Cheat!

D Daddy-long-legs – the one I dangled in front of Jake thinking it was a spider!

Me again! Who's the daddy?

E Earwig – we find one on the same bit of bark as the ants – good bit of bark, this. In fact, there seems to be a whole insect town centre under it. I always thought earwigs looked like caterpillars or grubs but Keziah identifies it right away with the help of Mrs Edmonds' lists.

I overheard you're doing a scavenger hunt, what fun! It's just that I'm a bit of an earwig

F Fern – ferns like moisture, which means they love sheltered, shaded areas, so this bit of woodland is the ideal location for them. We find quite a few about the place.

I'm so thirsty. Anyone got a glass of water?

G Grass – G is the first letter we do. We race off to get cracking and Keziah pulls a clump out

of the ground and says, 'Well, that's G sorted!'

H Hawthorn leaves – as much as I'd like to, I can't claim that we're able to identify a hawthorn leaf by ourselves. This is the first of Edmonds' planted clues. She's left a few different leaf bundles hidden about the place labelled with letter tags (the letter 'H' in this case).

She's also left tagged pictures of some other stuff lying around, like mushrooms, flowers and butterfly specimens, all neatly labelled with their corresponding letters. We reckon it'll take longer to look stuff up on the printed sheets and because time is of the essence we decide to find as much as possible on our own.

I Insect* – one of the ants from the vast collection we've uncovered!!!

J Juniper berries – these are also in a pre-tagged clump, which Edmonds has left hidden for us.

K is a tricky one . . .

K Kindling – a bunch of small twigs and sticks used to start a fire. Lighting campfires is a topic on one of the factsheets we received at our initial meeting and Jake remembers all about kindling from it. Nice one, Jake!

L Leaf – we are pretty much surrounded by them!

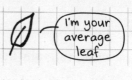

M Mud – we're stood on loads of the stuff!

Bog off!

N Nest – Keziah finds a small abandoned nest lying on the ground complete with empty eggshell. We decide we can use eggshell for E if we've identified the earwig incorrectly! We've got multiple options! How good are we?

Leave me alone, I'm nesting!

O Oak leaf – one of the few leaves we manage to recognise without a checklist because of its wiggly edges and the fact that as a kid I went through a phase where I was obsessed with acorns!! I actually collected them at one point and tried to make hats for my Playmobil characters from them!!

Nice hat!

Thanks!

P Pine cones – there are loads of these knocking about on the ground. I even find a closed one. I think that means it fell off in the rain.

Uh oh . . . it's gonna rain! Better close up

Q Queen ant* – we don't actually know for sure if this ant is the queen or not, but it looks a bit bigger than the others so we figure we'll give it a go as Q is not an easy one. I'm sure Edmonds has planted something beginning with 'Q' for us somewhere, but we don't want to waste our time looking for it!

I'm usually the one doing the picking!

R Red admiral butterfly – well, a picture of one left by Edmonds with an 'R' tag attached to it. Luckily Keziah knows what it is anyway so we don't even need to cross-check it on our handouts!

I'm not just any old butterfly, I'm an admiral! Edmonds would thoroughly approve.

S   Stick – from our kindling

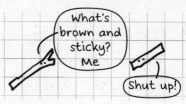

T   Twig – also from our kindling!

U   Ulmus minor leaf (from an English elm) – this one is the hardest letter to get! Jake spends a

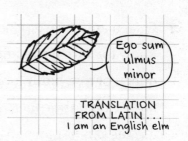

good while trying to identify it even though it's tagged with a 'U'! Doesn't help that the checklist isn't in alphabetical order – tricky when so many leaves look exactly the same!

V   Vine – I always thought vines had to grow grapes, but in fact they are any climbing or trailing plant and we've found a good few of them.

W   Woodlouse – hanging out with the ants under the bark!

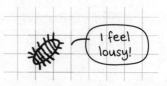

145

X Xylology – this is the study of wooded plants. It's on one of Edmonds' book lists so we put her whole tree checklist in for 'X'!!

Check out my trees!

Tree check-list

Y Yew leaf – yet another of Edmonds' pre-tagged leaf bunches. She's put quite a bit of effort into this scavenger hunt and all for the benefit of only six pupils. Does this woman not have a life?! As we romp through the undergrowth, clutching our specimen jars and magnifying glasses, we can't stop giggling. This scavenger hunt seems to be bringing me, Jake and Keziah back together again, and it's all thanks to Edmonds.

Hey! Yew!

Z As we rack our brains to think of something for the last letter of the alphabet, Keziah wanders off to search around in the foliage, insisting there must be a tagged picture of a zebra butterfly hidden somewhere.

Zebra butterfly

Wow, how did you know?

Lucky guess

Me and Jake laugh as we watch her frantically scrabbling about trying to find it in the closing minutes of the hunt.

'Hey,' he says, 'while I've got you alone.

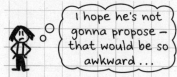

I hope he's not gonna propose — that would be so awkward . . .

There's something I've been meaning to tell you . . .'

But that's as far as he gets, because just as he's about to say it we're interrupted by Axel who's crouched under a nearby tree, chuckling to himself. He's clearly found something. We both bend down to take a closer look and there, hidden in the bushes, is a sleeping bag tagged with the letter 'Z' . . . well, 'Zzzzzzz' to be precise.

Is this a joke?! More mind games? A puzzle we're supposed to solve? Does it represent sleeping? Maybe it's something to do with hibernation? We aren't sure but all six of us note it down on our answer sheets.

Making our way back to Edmonds, I wonder whether insects go to sleep like us.

'Mrs Edmonds,' I ask, 'do insects go to sleep like us?'

'When insects aren't active and awake, they remain very still and don't respond to much,' she replies.

'This rest time is called "torpor".
It's a *bit* like sleep, I suppose.'

I had a terrible dream last night. Someone put me in a dish for a scavenger hunt

Oh dear

'Wonder if they have
dreams?' Suzie pipes up.

'Unlikely!' says Edmonds.

Mrs Edmonds knows an awful lot. She's pretty
cool.

We're all on a high after the scavenger hunt.
It's been such fun! Better still, our team won. Yay!
Edmonds is really impressed with us. The other
team found loads too, but not *every* letter like we
did! They managed to get *Xerocomus* though, which
is quite impressive. It's a type
of mushroom that she'd tagged
with the letter 'X'.

I've got the x factor!

Mrs Edmonds is delighted that we've all found

the sleeping bags.
She goes on to tell
us proudly that she
left them there as she
wanted to surprise us . . .

Surprise!

Because we've all done so well in the scavenger
hunt, she's going to take the six of us on our very
own camping trip in the wilderness! Not in the

wooded area next door to the school . . . but in a
proper forest!!!

OMG!! We're all SO excited! This will be brilliant!
Me, Jake and Keziah high-five each other. We
decide the three of us will go shopping together
on Saturday to get supplies for the trip. Suzie looks
over, annoyed – she seems instantly jealous that
I've reunited with my friends. For the last couple of
days, she's been nagging me about going shopping
to buy new clothes for the Aliana
gig, but I keep making excuses to
get out of it. I'm going shopping
with my *real* friends now.

That's when I remember that Jake was trying to
tell me something before in the woods. I wander
over to him as we're grabbing all our stuff to go
home.

'Hey! What was it you were going to tell me
earlier?' I ask. He looks all serious. But before he
can answer, Suzie calls over.

'Babes, I just had the most horrific thought! What if the camping trip clashes with our Aliana gig?! That'd be totally awkward! We really should check with Mrs Edmonds. I mean, Aliana has been the highlight of our social calendar for ages!'

She keeps on talking but I can't hear it any more. I can't hear anything. I've tuned out and I'm focusing on Jake, who has just realised that I've given the Aliana ticket to Suzie and not to him. He looks wounded, shocked and hurt. Tears well up in his eyes.

'I . . . I . . . thought you hadn't given the ticket away yet,' he stutters, staring at me in total disbelief.

'We arranged it a while back,' says Suzie, twisting the knife. 'Sorry, Jakey-pie – did you want to come as well? I'm afraid we only have the two tickets.'

I stand there dumbfounded, unable to say anything. I go to open my mouth and explain but it's too late . . . Jake has gone.

CHAPTER 13

Shopping Centre Disaster!

Jake is in a really bad mood with me for the rest of the week. I figure he won't be able to keep it up though, especially as we sit next to each other in class. Once he stops being annoyed with me, I'll fix everything. I'll explain to him that I actually *sold* the ticket to Suzie in exchange for the much-needed funds to stop me missing out on Forest Club. Forest Club: the one thing that currently gives me enjoyment in my otherwise dismal life.

Surely he'll understand that? It was simply a financial transaction. My relationship with Suzie is purely business. Maybe I should just give him the other Aliana ticket and then everything would be OK again . . . ? I don't even know how much I want to go to the gig with Suzie anyway. Suzie must have picked that exact moment to let Jake know she was coming to the concert with me to upset him. I reckon she did it on purpose as she was jealous that we'd just made up.

It's going to be tricky but I'm determined to smooth things over. I just need the chance to explain myself . . .

But Jake's mood doesn't improve. He's back to giving me one-word answers to everything and going out of his way to avoid me.

No lunch together, no walking home, no lending me his sharpener in class, and when I ask him if I can borrow it, he pretends not to hear me! We've sunk to new lows.

Go on, Jake . . . let her borrow me. It's obvious you can hear her — no one wants a blunt pencil!

He doesn't even look me in the face once the whole of Friday, despite me trying to catch his eye at every possible opportunity. He'd beat Axel hands down in the 'No Eye Contact' World Championships right now.

1st place in the Floor-staring World Cup goes to Jake!

Why is he not taking the cup?

He can't see it — he's too busy looking at the floor!

I decide to go round to his house after school and confront him. His mum will let me up to his room and then I'll have him captive. He'll have to hear me out.

Uh oh . . . can't remember where I put the keys to the handcuffs!

I ring the doorbell but when his mum answers she seems surprised to see me.

'I thought Jake was with you at Forest Club,' she says, confused. 'He said there were meetings till late every day after school in the weeks leading up to the big camping trip.'

'Oh yeah,' I say unconvincingly. 'I forgot!'

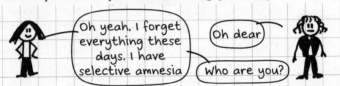

What on earth is going on?! Where is Jake? Why isn't he at home? Why's he lying to his mum? Have I pushed him over the edge? Has he run away? Is he abroad already? Is he remembering to put sun cream on? My mind is running away from me. Of course he isn't! Whatever he's up to, he's been doing it every day this week.

When I get home, I decide to email him on Dad's computer but get no reply. I send another and another . . . still nothing.

I feel like a stalker. How late is he gonna stay out?! At bedtime, he still hasn't responded to me! UGH! SO ANNOYING. I'LL CALL HIM AND GET TO THE BOTTOM OF THIS IF IT'S THE LAST THING I DO . . .

I don't get to call him in the end as Roubi is on the phone the whole night and I'm so exhausted from my long week that I fall asleep. I'll try him tomorrow.

Zzzzzzzebra butterfly

The next morning when I actually get to try him, the phone rings out for ages – very normal in Jake's house. After what feels like a year, his younger brother Will answers.

Hello

Oh no!

Will?! Oh no! Not Will! He can't stop talking at the best of times! People have rung Jake's house before and have had to put up with Will babbling on for a good fifteen minutes before they even realise that no one else in the house is going to notice and intercept the call. He literally talks to complete strangers on the street!

Anyone and everyone! He can talk about anything . . .

Random lady in street

The ERM was the preferred method of equating currencies blah blah

'Mum says Tesco is launching a new own-brand healthy-eating no-carb range,' he says. 'She's going to try it. I like their own-brand prawn cocktail

crisps best. They're better than all
the other ones . . .'

'Will, I really need to speak to Jake . . .' I interject.

But it's no use . . .

'Did you know that prawn cocktail crisps are
made without any prawns? I don't actually like
prawns. My favourite food is peanut butter. The
smooth stuff, not the crunchy
stuff, because the crunchy
stuff gets stuck in your teeth.
I lost a tooth last week . . .'

I might have to give up on this. I'll try one last
time before hanging up.

'Will! Is Jake there?!' I say.

'Huh? Jake? No, he's out. He's always out these
days. I wish I could go out more. Mum never lets me
out on my own or without a coat. I got a new coat
the other day. It has Super Mario on it and Yoshi but
not Luigi. Do you think that's strange?'

I've wasted three-quarters
of an hour of my life already.
I NEED to get off this call!

'Hey,' I say quickly before he can start talking
about anything else, 'how was Disneyland?'

'Disneyland? That's in America, although there is one in France. And Japan. I've never been but I have been to Balls and Bounce, the new soft play place by the retail park. The ball pit is really big and it has giant foam shapes in it as well as balls and numbers and letters too . . .'

Another fifteen minutes pass before I finally get Will off the phone. Where on earth is Jake? Maybe Keziah will know. I call her but she isn't home either. Where is everyone?!

Roubi

is going shopping with her friends this morning. I decide to tag along to see if there's anything I need for the camping trip, as shopping with Jake and Keziah won't be happening now. Roubi and her friends couldn't be less enthusiastic about having me – 'the little sister' – in tow.

To be fair, Mum kind

of forced her to take me along. She gave us five
pounds each as bribery so we could have lunch
in the shopping centre's brand-
new food hall. Break the bank, why
don't you, Mum?! That place is SO
expensive. We probably won't even
be able to buy a peanut!

Menu	
Burger	£100
Chips	£50
Drink	£20
Peanut	£60
20% service charge	

I make sure I have a
massive breakfast before we
leave so I can save the money
and put it towards the bike
I'll never be able to afford.

Bike = £100

Money collected = so far	£25 voucher + £5 lunch money
	£30 total

Still needed
£100 − £30 = £70

I also bring extra
food in my coat
pocket to snack on
in case I get hungry.
Always thinking
ahead!

Cookie's pocket

Mini Cheddars

It's snug in here

Yes, there's loads of us
in here. Cookie's always
thinking ahead . . . when
it comes to food

'Cookie, babes!' I hear a voice call out as we come
around a corner in the shopping centre. There,
waving frantically in my direction, is Suzie. She's
out shopping with her mum,
who is wearing the brightest
pink coat I've ever seen.

brightest
pink ever

'We're getting stuff for the camping trip,' Suzie says. 'You should join us! Wouldn't it be funny if we got matching stuff?'

Before I even have time to speak, Suzie's mum says, 'Great idea! We can drop you back home later, Cookie!' and Roubi replies, 'Perfect! That way you can go to all the right shops instead of us dragging you wherever we go. Have fun! See you later!'

And with that, Roubi and her friends disappear off in a flash. They couldn't have got rid of me any quicker.

Judging from the number of bags they're carrying, Suzie and her mum have already bought half the shopping centre. It's like they can't spend money fast enough!!

In the first shop we go into, Suzie's mum buys her a bright pink Bluetooth speaker without even pausing to think about it or looking at the price.

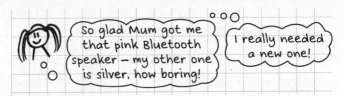

In the next shop, she buys Suzie a pop-up tent, despite the fact that Edmonds said she's going to provide everyone with tents. Why buy something you don't need?! What a waste!

The tent is perfect for Suzie though, as it doesn't need to be assembled, you just open the case and it pops up! No brain power necessary!

They ask me if I'm going to buy anything so I lie and tell them I'm gonna buy stuff online instead.

While we're in the shopping centre we decide to stop for lunch. Suzie kindly reminds me that I'm still fasting. Thanks, Suzie! I sit there eyeing up the pack of Mini Cheddars poking out of my coat pocket while Suzie and her mum each wolf down a hamburger, fries and milkshake.

I'm starving. I'll need to end the holy month of Ramadan before the camping trip or it will be unbearable. For some reason, every time I try to tell Suzie it's over I chicken out. It's become such a big lie now that I don't know how to get out of it. How is it that I can lie so easily and convincingly about stuff when it's spontaneous but pre-planning lies is really difficult?!

Suzie's mum is really impressed that I'm still fasting (!) and says it's great that I have so much determination and drive (which I definitely do to be able to keep up this whole pretence). She tells me I'll go far (which I definitely will . . . I hope.)

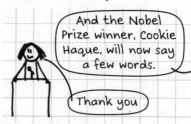

Just as we're about to get up and leave the food hall, who should come and sit down at the table next to us but . . . Jake AND Keziah! We spot each other at the same time. Keziah tries to smile but Jake pulls a face and comments snidely: 'Hi Cookie! Out with your NBFF, are you?! How sweet. That means "New Best Friend Forever" by the way.'

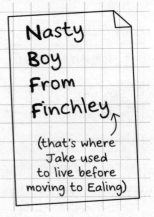

Nasty
Boy
From
Finchley

(that's where Jake used to live before moving to Ealing)

I can't believe they've gone on our shopping trip WITHOUT ME! Traitors! Again!! Well, this time they're welcome to each other!

CHAPTER 14

Camping in the Mud

The camping trip has been organised for the coming weekend. We bring our permission slips in on Monday and the six of us receive a letter containing all the information we need to know and a list of everything we're required to bring with us. Wow! This is becoming real. How fun! We're going on a camping trip with NO adults! Well, apart from Edmonds, but she's kind of one of us now!

The whole class are crowding around in the classroom to look at the list of camping essentials before afternoon lessons begin.

List of camping essentials	
• Tent	• Trainers
• Torch	• Swimwear
• Sleeping bag	• Thermals
• PJs	• 3 x change of clothes
• Toiletries	• Insect repellent
• Waterproof coat	• Towel
• Walking boots	

'You'll be sleeping in sleeping bags?' says Tayo. 'Amazing! You should totally sneak into one tent and have a midnight feast when Edmonds is asleep!'

I like this idea but it might be tricky what with Jake not speaking to me, and Keziah not saying much either. She isn't totally ignoring me like he is, but she's definitely being colder than usual.

Jake has obviously brainwashed her against me! They probably both think I'd pre-arranged to go shopping with Suzie – not that I'd been ruthlessly dumped on her at the last minute by my heartless sister. They'll be sorry when they realise they haven't got the full picture and see how unfairly they've been treating me.

164

In class, everyone seems to be getting FOMO over the whole F Factor thing. FOMO factor!

Some of them even ask Edmonds if they can come on the camping trip too, but she tells them it's only for us Forest Clubbers. Her 'gang'. There's a waiting list in case any of us turn out to be busy that bank holiday weekend and can't go or if someone has to pull out at the last minute. But we've all cleared our diaries. Mine never has anything in it anyway!

We're all really looking forward to it. If it's even a tenth as fun as the scavenger hunt, it'll be so worth it.

'Do we have to take matches and eat off a fire?' asks Alison.

'Edmonds will bring special fire-lighting sticks and we'll probably get plates to eat off,' replies Jake.

'Plates?! Luxury!' giggles Keziah.

Great! He and Keziah are now having fun with

Alison instead of me. What if he starts becoming friendly with ALL the others, including Suzie? Then I'll be left completely friendless on the trip. Maybe I *should* be best buddies with Suzie? After all, she's the only one communicating with me normally at the moment!

On Saturday morning, we all assemble in the school car park. It's strange seeing the school on a weekend. It's so lifeless and empty compared to the chaotic hustle and bustle we're used to on a weekday.

Everyone's parents have come to wave them off. Jake's mum is there with nearly the whole family: talkative Will, his sister Helen and their baby brother Archie are all present and correct, as Edmonds would say (it's an army term, you see). It's like a family outing, only his dad isn't with them.

It's a bit weird he's not there as his dad's the type that loves barbecues and camping trips. This is his kind of thing! He's the sort of man who would look more at home in a harness and helmet scaling a cliff face than sat on a sofa.

He's probably given Jake a pep talk about the trip, unlike my parents who just wanted to give me a snack bag, which I declined. It had enough in it to feed an army – Edmonds would have approved. They also offered to collect me in the evening so I could sleep at home overnight!! Errrr. . . that kind of goes against the whole point of camping!!!! Duh!!!

We all pile into the school minibus and wave our goodbyes. Luckily, it's a beautiful crisp sunny day – perfect camping weather. Everyone is in good spirits considering half of us have fallen out with each other!

Edmonds tries to get us to have a sing-along on the journey. 'A thousand green bottles sitting on the wall!' she begins in a gruff, deep voice – it's mildly scary. We all duck down out of sight so she can't see us in the rear-view mirror.

As hardly any of us are speaking to each other, getting us all to sing together would be nothing short of miraculous. After ages, we stop at a service station and are allowed to look around the mini arcade, go to the toilet, eat our packed lunches and check out the magazines in the newsagent's. I can't shake Suzie, who is making me look at an Aliana Tiny fanzine.

As the two of us end up hanging out together for the entire lunch stop, I don't get to eat anything.

The rest of the minibus journey is uneventful. By the time we reach the forest, everyone's fallen asleep in the back of the bus and it's chucking it down with rain.

'Welcome to the forest!! Everyone out!!' booms Edmonds at about a thousand decibels. 'Tents up! Quick smart!'

This is a rude awakening from the warmth and

dryness of the van
that had rocked us
gently to sleep . . .

We're callously
thrown into the miserable sheet rain, which is

pelting down onto the muddy
forest floor.

Ping! Suzie's tent
pops up instantly.

'Get in, Cookie!' she yells over the
torrential downpour.

I want to help the others. This trip won't be
fun without us all getting along. Jake obviously
doesn't want my help; Keziah seems to be feeling
bad for Jake; Alison is jealous of Suzie being nice
to me; and Axel is even less likely to make eye
contact in a level-ten onslaught of pouring rain.
It'll be impossible to get the cooperation and
communication needed to erect a tent with this lot.

'Come on!' shouts Suzie. 'Hurry up!'

I leap into her tent. It's safe, dry, warm and pink
(very pink – in fact, it's
like being inside a giant
watermelon).

Meanwhile, everyone else runs around outside like headless chickens trying to put their own tents up. Alison looks as though she's crying but there's so much rain that it's hard to tell for sure.

Is it raining? I hadn't noticed

I feel terrible in here with just me and Suzie. The others will hate me even more now. But this isn't my fault. Jake is the one being funny with me! Mind you, I needn't worry too much about them hating me – you can bet they'll all be getting angry with each other out there in the rain and mud, trying to sort out which tent peg goes where, while Edmonds barks orders at them. I'm well out of it.

Tent peg j2 should go in hole k4, I think

What?! Give me those instructions

PHEW!

Edmonds will probably make us come out and help any moment now. It surely isn't the army way not to muck in together with the rest of your platoon or regiment or whatever. We wait but she doesn't come. We seem to have been left to it. After about fifteen minutes or so our curiosity gets the better of us and we decide to peek outside to see what's going on. We pull down the zip at the front of the tent and poke our heads out to have a good look . . .

The others are soaking wet right through but are all in hysterics. They're laughing uncontrollably at the hilarity of the situation, slipping and sliding about in the mud like something out of a Tom and Jerry cartoon. It's a funny sight – they're drenched right

through, with their hair clinging to their faces and wet clothes clinging to their bodies.

I want join in but at the same time feel annoyed that they're sharing this moment without ME! They're clearly having the time of their lives and I don't like it one little bit. Suzie pulls the zip up and we retreat back inside the tent.

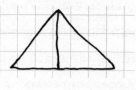

'Urgh! They'll be sorry,' she says. 'They'll get sick rolling around in all that bacteria. Come on – let's eat chocolate and listen to music and gossip while they bathe in the muck like pigs!'

'Yeah, gross,' I say, secretly jealous I'm not bathing in muck with them.

'Oh no! It's not dark yet – you can't eat!' she says, 'Ramakuh, remember!' She pulls a slab of butterscotch-flecked chocolate out of her backpack, breaks off a row of cubes and casually tosses it into her mouth. 'No matter! Only a couple of hours before the sun goes down. Hang on in there, babycakes!'

If only I could come clean and tell her! But when I open my mouth nothing comes out so I just sit there in silence.

She swipes through some music on her tablet, taps on the song of choice and grins as she turns up the volume.

'Be who you am and am who you be, say what you like, you'll never be me,' Aliana Tiny sings out from Suzie's hot-pink Bluetooth speaker as she croons along. Oh no! Worst music ever! She chomps on more chocolate and starts busting out dance moves.

This is awful! Jake will think I'm rubbing it in his face on purpose. How will I ever make up with him now?

CHAPTER 15

Ghost Stories

When it finally stops raining and the others have changed into dry clothes and fully recovered from the tent-pitching caper, Mrs Edmonds gives us a tour of the area and a quick rundown of what's what.

To the left you'll find trees next to some trees, and behind some more trees. To the right you'll find much the same. Make sure you don't lose your way among the trees!

She then tells us that we're going to light a fire. The prospect of a proper campfire to gather around telling stories and cooking food is an exciting one! It'll be just like in films and on telly. Keziah is the only one who's a bit nervous, as she knows this means it's going to be night-time soon and there are no Winnie-the-Pooh digital alarm clocks or night lights in the forest. Just darkness.

Where's the plug socket? I need to plug in my straighteners!

OMG – that would be amazing . . . I could plug in my night light!

I, on the other hand, can't wait for it to turn dark so we can have dinner because I'm absolutely STARVING. Everyone else ate lunch except for me so I can't wait to get stuck into my evening meal! I'm literally counting

179 minutes
178 minutes
177 minutes . . .

down the minutes.

Lighting a fire looks so much easier on TV. In real life it's nearly impossible.

What do you mean, you can't just rub two sticks together?

Things probably aren't helped by the fact that everything is damp. Luckily, Edmonds has brought loads of ground sheets, so we put them down all over the place. It's a bit like having an outdoor carpet. We can sit and roll around on the floor quite comfortably!

Can we all just take our shoes off? I don't want to get the groundsheet dirty!

Lighting the fire is another matter though. We have to find a bit of flat ground that isn't too wet and then create the fire triangle! Oxygen, fuel and heat – the three components necessary for fire. Take any of these away and your fire goes out.

My dad runs a restaurant and a pan once caught fire in the kitchen. The chef put it out by turning the cooker off (taking away the fuel) and covering it with a tea towel (taking away the oxygen) – plus the tea towel was damp (taking away the heat). Triple whammy!!

Mrs Edmonds tells me and Axel to get a bucket of water from the lake nearby in case our fire gets out of hand. I know this is just Edmonds wanting us to be all survivalist and army-like because I noticed she actually brought a fire extinguisher with her in one of her bags! Next, she'll be making us live off the land!

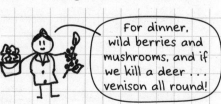

For dinner, wild berries and mushrooms, and if we kill a deer . . . venison all round!

Once we all settle down, our camp feels really cosy and inviting. The fire takes a while to get going properly as the wood has to have lots of air gaps in between to keep a good supply of oxygen. In the end, Edmonds has to help us build it. We light it with a magnesium flint stick, which we rub against a steel stick to create a hot spark and kick it all off. Jake says it looks like a dragon sneezing, which is pretty spot on!

Achoo

Hope they're not joking at my expense. I've got a terrible cold and keep burning things down by mistake!

I try not to laugh. Even though we're all having fun, Jake is continuing to ignore me.

It's still light by the time we start making dinner. Why so early? How will I avoid eating till it turns dark? I pretend to get obsessive over picking up bits of rubbish from the forest floor so as not to join in with the meal. I watch on as vegetarian sausages, baked beans, and bread and butter triangles are dished out and pray that Suzie won't announce I'm fasting. Keziah, Jake and Axel know that Ramadam was back in May, so it will definitely look weird if Suzie says anything. Alison probably doesn't have a clue – I bet she doesn't even know what fasting is!

Luckily, Suzie goes off to disinfect her hands with antibacterial gel. While she's away, I quickly declare that I'll eat my food after I've finished picking up litter. This way it won't look weird to Suzie or the others that I'm not eating.

'Once it's dark I won't be able to see anything,' I say. 'The planet won't save itself! I can't relax till I've finished. You guys carry on. Won't be long.'

'What a wonderful example, Cookie! Well done!' cries Mrs Edmonds.

It's painful waiting for the sun to go down, listening to the others munching away as my stomach groans on at me.

After about three-quarters of an hour it finally gets dark, which means fake fasting is over for the day. At last, I can eat! Hurray! Sheer jubilance! I could've eaten the whole campsite at that moment.

I race over to the others, my stomach begging me for food. I put down my bag of rubbish and say, 'I hope you haven't been littering, gang!'

Mrs Edmonds chuckles away as though I've said the most hilarious joke she's ever heard.

My face falls. 'Oh! There's only one sausage and a few baked beans left.' (I count them – there are only fourteen beans in total!)

At least they left you a sausage!

yeah . . . so ungrateful!

Still, on the bright side, it's the best vegetarian sausage and fourteen baked beans I've had in my entire life. If only I could have had ten times as much! For pudding we each have some toasted marshmallows, which Edmonds frugally rations out, one by one. I could have happily polished off the whole bag, but, hey, the night is young!

Come back and eat the rest of us later . . . we'll be waiting!

Being in the great outdoors is amazing! We are at one with nature. The fire gives us warmth and light, crackling away blissfully against the night sky. We are all relishing the moment. Sheer joy!

'Mrs Edmonds,' asks Axel, 'when you were in the army did you ever kill anyone?'

'It would be foolish to say . . .' replies Edmonds. 'What happens in combat stays in combat!'

'Huh?!' says Suzie.

'It means I can't tell you or I'd have to kill you!' jokes Edmonds. At least I hope she's joking . . .

Hope no one digs them up

Edmonds has been in combat?! No way! She's probably been in war zones and everything!! She can really handle herself, which makes us all feel safe in her company. It's getting quite creepy in the forest now. The later and darker it gets, the stranger the noises and shadows are.

That Mrs Edmonds is really scary

These shadows are really scary

Yeah, she's terrifying!

'Can you tell us a story of one of your army adventures?' asks Jake.

'Well, OK then, seeing as it's you six,' says Edmonds. She looks around before she begins, as though she's about to tell us a state secret and wants to check no one else is listening in.

Mama

Shhh . . . I want to hear what Edmonds has to say . . .

'One day, my troops were all at base, sitting around a fire much like this one, in the middle of an unknown territory . . .'

'Huh?' says Suzie.

'They were somewhere they didn't know,' explains Keziah.

Oh brother . . . we're in for a long night if every sentence is going to need explaining!

Once upon a time? Huh? What does that even mean?

Edmonds goes on to tell us how some of her company or battalion or whatever you call it had wandered off and disappeared, never to be seen again. The locals said later that they'd probably been eaten by the native man-eating ghosts!

Hmmm . . . only children? I was hoping for a big, fat man

'Right!' says Edmonds, getting up. 'Just going to put some things away in the van and then it's bedtime.' She disappears off.

'Man-eating ghosts?' says Alison, turning pale.

I roll my eyes. Edmonds blatantly made that story up to stop us wandering off on our own in the night.

'Don't be ridiculous!' says Jake. 'Ghosts don't exist!'

'And they certainly don't eat people!' chimes in Keziah.

'I really don't feel well,' says Alison. She doesn't look well either. 'I think I'm gonna be sick!' she cries, running to the loo. When I say loo, it's more of a dilapidated hut with a hole in the ground.

Moments later, we hear a piercing cry echo through the forest. Alison runs back at top speed, screaming.

'I saw a ghost!' she splutters, shaken up and trying to catch her breath.

'Where?' asks Axel, laughing.

'In the toilet. It was a floating, glowing head without a body!' Alison is hysterical.

'You must have imagined it,' says Keziah.

'I know what I saw,' she protests. 'I'm not stupid.'

'You're winding us up!' says Jake.

'She wouldn't do that!' says Suzie, defending her best friend (well, her ex-best friend). She knows Alison better than all of us and is convinced she's telling the truth. To be fair, Alison isn't really the type to trick people, unless she's just playing along with Suzie. But Suzie definitely isn't in on this.

'Was it inside the actual toilet?' asks Suzie.

Ugh ... can't reach the loo roll. Don't you hate it when that happens?

'Doing a wee!' adds Jake, giggling.

'No! It was in the hut thing that houses the toilet,' sobs Alison.

It's getting pretty dark and scary now and the six of us are unsure what to do about Alison's outburst. She really has lost it.

'I'll get Edmonds,' says Axel. 'She'll check it out!'

We wait and reassure Alison.

'I've never liked the dark!' says Keziah, trying to be helpful.

What is going on? Has Alison made it up or imagined it? It can't be true, can it?!

At that moment, Axel dashes back towards us.

'Edmonds has gone!' he says. 'She's not packing stuff into the minibus and she's not in her tent either. She's gone!'

CHAPTER 16

Actual Ghosts

Where is Mrs Edmonds? Has she been taken by a man-eating ghost?! What if she's stumbled over a tree root and knocked herself unconscious? Or maybe she's just gone to get some more water from the lake? The fire has become pretty big and will need to be put out for the night. But what if she's tripped and fallen in?

Is the lake deep? I know people swim in it as it has a ramshackle building next to it with a 'Forest Outdoor Swimming Club' timetable pinned to the door. What if she's drowning?! Surely you have to be able to swim to be in the army?

ARMY RECRUITMENT INTERVIEW . . .

Can you swim?

No, but I have my tank driver's licence and can hit a moving target from a mile away

Alison is nearly hyperventilating now.

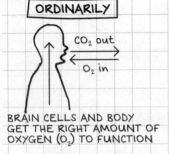

ORDINARILY	HYPERVENTILATING

CO_2 out
O_2 in

BRAIN CELLS AND BODY GET THE RIGHT AMOUNT OF OXYGEN (O_2) TO FUNCTION

more CO_2 out
more O_2 in

THE CARBON DIOXIDE (CO_2) LEVELS IN YOUR BLOOD DROP TOO LOW SO THE BLOOD VESSELS SUPPLYING THE BRAIN NARROW, CAUSING LIGHT-HEADEDNESS

Breathing furiously, she stutters, 'Worse still, I . . . I . . .' She stops, unable to continue, much to Suzie's annoyance.

'You . . . what?!' snaps Suzie impatiently. We're all getting frustrated now.

'Worse still, I . . . I . . .' continues Alison. 'It sounds ridiculous but I . . . I'm sure I heard the ghost call my name as I ran away!!!'

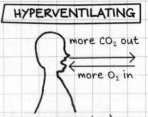

Alison!!

She's quivering and tears are streaming down her cheeks. The poor girl is in a real state.

What's she crying about? We're not real

Wonder who on earth that was!

'How could it have known your name?!' Jake bursts out laughing. 'What am I talking about? Ghosts don't even exist!!!!'

What on earth is going on?!! Is there a name-calling ghost out there?! As if.

'Alison!' a distant voice calls out from somewhere in the bushes. We all freeze. Alison starts screaming. Suzie looks annoyed – she clearly isn't pleased that Alison is currently the centre of attention. Suzie isn't used to that.

Huh? Why is everyone focusing on Alison so much when I'm here? This is unheard of!

'Alison!' repeats the deep, gruff voice . . . but it isn't the voice of a man-eating ghost, although I must admit I don't know what a man-eating ghost's voice sounds like.

Howfore art thou? I am a man-eating ghost. Does thou want to be eaten?

No thanks! I don't believe in ghosts – but I didn't think you'd be so posh sounding!

I do know this voice though . . . it belongs to Mrs Edmonds!

'Alison!' she says, emerging from the bushes. You really should knock before entering the toilet – there's no lock, you know.'

'Huh?' says Suzie, confused.

'You're the ghost!' grins Axel.

'Not a ghost,' replies Edmonds. 'Just an innocent civilian trying to use the toilet in peace.'

'Told you so,' crows Jake, 'there's no such thing as ghosts!'.

'Jake's right,' I say, hoping he'll respond to me and that this could be a bit of an ice-breaker for us. But he doesn't – he's still ignoring me.

'It can't be. You can't be,' sobs Alison. 'I saw it with my own eyes. There was a glowing head in the dark.'

'You mean there was an innocent civilian in dark clothes in a dark toilet with her head illuminated by the light of her mobile phone!' snaps Edmonds matter-of-factly.

GLOWING HEAD IN THE DARK

REALITY: EDMONDS IN THE LOO

'Huh?' says Suzie.

'Illuminated means lit up!' explains Keziah, giggling.

'By the way, whoever goes to the toilet next – take this with you,' says Edmonds, holding up a loo roll. 'I finished the last one.'

I'm the last toilet roll – use me sparingly. Think of the environment!

We all laugh. It's funny. The whole thing is funny. Although Alison looks visibly upset that Suzie is joining in and laughing too, eventually she does see the funny side. Better still, Alison reckons she's finally got over her fear of  ghosts!

We have a big day ahead of us tomorrow. Edmonds says we'll be doing all sorts of outdoor activities and challenges. Exciting! (I think . . .) I'm hoping it'll be more stuff like the minibeast hotel and the scavenger hunt as opposed to an army assault course or a ten-mile cross-country run.

After we've brushed our teeth and put on our pyjamas, we all get into our tents ready for our first night's sleep under the stars.

Lying there, looking up at the hot-pink fabric ceiling, I really hope Keziah is OK. It's so dark outside. The sky is pitch black – there's no moon in sight. The glowing embers left behind from the fire add little if any light to that of the few stars present

in the sky tonight. Ordinarily, I'd be reassuring
Keziah right now, but because I was dragged into
Suzie's tent during the rainstorm, Keziah has ended
up sharing with Alison instead of me. I say dragged,
but to be honest I wasn't complaining during the

downpour when
I was dry and
everyone else
was getting
drenched!

Edmonds has her own tent and Jake is sharing
with Axel. It's been so much fun around the
campfire this evening. My only regret is that Jake
is still annoyed with me. I curl up into a ball in
the top half of my sleeping bag and think about

everything that's
happened. It's hard
to block out all the
forest sounds: owls,
insects and other
odd noises.

Before long, Suzie nods off and I feel lonely and
a bit frightened. I'm sure I can hear shuffling and
crunching outside. I stay dead still in the comfort

of my sleeping bag. When the noise
gets really close, I dare to peek out
through scrunched-up eyes and spot
a scary shadow looming over the
entrance of the tent.

A bright torch light shines in my face and a head
pokes in: 'You up, Cookie?'

It's Keziah! Yay! She says she can't get to sleep.

'Quick! Get in!' I laugh with relief. 'I can't sleep
either. And dim that light a bit! We'll all go blind!'

Keziah carries that torch with her everywhere
when it gets dark. Flashlight
is an understatement –
flood light is more like it!
It's ridiculously bright!

'OK, OK!' she says, dimming the torch. 'I've really
gotta ditch this "scared of the dark" thing, haven't I?
Especially now that Alison's over her fear of ghosts!'

'I doubt she is!'
I say. 'I thought we
were gonna have to
call an ambulance
after the toilet-
ghost incident.'

We laugh. I'm so happy to see my best friend in the whole wide world. I've really missed Keziah – it's time for a proper catch-up.

She grabs my stripy anorak and we huddle up together. Keziah says she's missed me too and that it feels like I'm hanging out with Suzie all the time these days. I explain how the whole Suzie friendship was accidental, and that I *sold* the ticket to Suzie – I didn't give it to her. I point out that I only did it so I could get the twenty-five-pound Forest Club joining fee. I also tell her how last week's shopping trip had come about totally by chance. She giggles. We both do – pretty loudly!

Suzie shuffles, and for a second we're worried we've woken her up. Luckily we haven't. I tell Keziah about fake Ramadan and we chuckle away as I recount all the times I've had to eat in hiding or starve myself as others scoffed their food down in front of me.

Just then, my stomach lets out a huge growl as if to remind me I've only had one sausage, fourteen baked beans and three marshmallows for dinner. I need to eat soon before I die of starvation.

What you need is a midnight feast!

'Poor you!' says Keziah. 'What you need is a midnight feast!'

'I've got an idea!' I say, jumping up. 'I'll eat the leftover marshmallows! Edmonds put them in that tin next to the fire. If they're there all night an animal will probably eat them anyway! Wait here!'

Who ate all the marshmallows last night?

Errr . . . just doing the responsible thing so they didn't go to waste. It's not cos I actually wanted to eat them!

I pull a spare ground sheet over me for warmth and gingerly make my way over to the marshmallows, tiptoeing across the twigs and stones that cover the

twig — Ugh that girl just trod on me — Shut up — stick

forest floor so as to be as quiet as possible.

As I open the hinged lid of the marshmallow tin it lets out an almighty creak. The marshmallows look unbelievably good! Soft, puffy clouds of joy saying 'Eat me!' to my willing tummy.

DON'T EAT US, PLEASE!!

Without pausing for breath, I start shovelling them into my mouth and chomping away loudly. Yum! I hear a zip open but can't stop gorging on the marshmallows. Suddenly, there's a high-pitched, piercing scream. I turn around to see Alison staring at me in pure terror. Behind her are Axel and Suzie, who are screaming too. Then to my utter disbelief Jake appears behind them and joins in as well. They all think I'm a ghost.

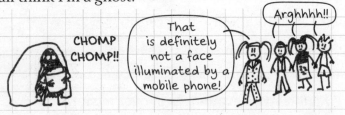

Covered in my ground sheet with marshmallow powder all over my face, accompanied by gobbling noises and the sound of the tin creaking, I totally understand why they think that. Even I'm a bit scared of me!

I stop munching and look up at them. The sheet falls off me. Everyone is relieved. We hear loud grunting and shuffling noises coming from Edmonds' direction. Giggling, we all race back into Suzie's tent as it's the closest. Thankfully it's just Edmonds rolling over in her sleeping bag. She starts

snoring loudly – she's slept
through the whole thing!!

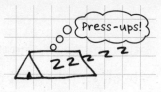

By now, the six of us are back in Suzie's tent
laughing at the ridiculousness of the situation. We're
doubled over in hysterics thinking about it. It takes us
a good few minutes to recompose ourselves. Alison,
however, still looks like the living dead – all pale
and disturbed. I must have been a pretty terrifying
sight. Even Jake 'I'm not scared of anything and
don't believe in ghosts' Kay got a fright.

'Thought you didn't believe in
ghosts, Jakey-pie,' I say, teasing him.

But Jake is still blanking me . . .

'Cheer up, Alison!' says Axel, looking at the
ground. 'We're all scared of something! I can't
bear heights, remember? I bet there'll be a tree-
climbing challenge tomorrow and I'll probably have
a meltdown too!'

We all laugh. Axel is trying to be helpful but
it sounds more like an insult! Poor
Alison doesn't look like she'll get over
her fear of ghosts any time soon.

'Hey!' says Suzie. 'Now you're all here, I reckon
it's time for a midnight feast.' She rubs on some

antibac hand gel, and then from out of her bag grabs the same huge slab of butterscotch chocolate she'd been eating earlier while I starved.

I pull my sleeping bag around me to make a bit of space for everyone to sit down, and feel something nestling right at the bottom of it. I delve inside only to find the snack bag that Mum had tried to give me earlier today. She'd snuck it in and, boy, was I glad of it now.

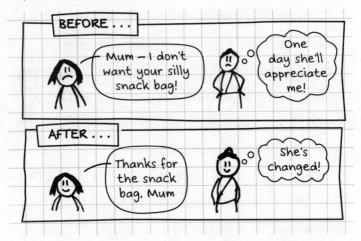

BEFORE...

Mum — I don't want your silly snack bag!

One day she'll appreciate me!

AFTER...

Thanks for the snack bag, Mum

She's changed!

'Wow! You've got enough in there to feed an army!' says Axel.

'Or a Forest Club!' jokes Keziah.

I really do! Mum definitely doesn't skimp when it comes to feeding people.

'Good thinking ahead!!' says Alison

'Thanks!' I say, taking the praise.

'Be prepared!' laughs Suzie. 'Isn't that an army motto? Edmonds would be proud!'

'Errr . . . I think you'll find that's actually the Boy Scouts' motto,' says Keziah, laughing.

We spread all the goodies out over the floor of the tent and tuck in. We feast away merrily into the early hours as Edmonds snores away contentedly in her tent, completely oblivious. It's been such a good night, apart from the fact that Jake still isn't talking to me. Something I'm determined to change . . .

After everyone has gone back to their own tents, I drift off thinking about the whole Jake situation. I wish we could just talk to each other!

Keziah seems to be back on side now, so that's good, and tomorrow is a new day and a fresh beginning . . .

CHAPTER 17

Zipwire!

Ding-a-ling-a-ling-a-ling!

I hear a bell ringing in the distance. My head feels heavy. Where am I? Is this a dream? Am I in the school playground? Is that the fire alarm? It takes me a while to come round from my slumber and gain consciousness, as the bell continues to grow louder and louder.

DING-A-LING-A-LING-A-LING-A-LING!

I soon realise this is no dream. I awake confused and disorientated to a booming voice. And then I remember – we're in the middle of a forest. I look up to see Mrs Edmonds standing over us in our hot-pink tent.

'Time to get up, ladies!' she calls out. 'Nothing like a morning swim to get your blood flowing! Costumes on! The day is dawning! *Carpe diem!*'

Carpe diem?! I glance at Suzie's alarm clock. It's 5.30 a.m.!! We couldn't have got to sleep till about 1.30 a.m. after last night's antics. I know *carpe diem* is Latin for 'seize the day' but can't we seize the day when it's actually DAYTIME?! It's barely even started to get light outside. Worse still, we're all so

groggy and out of it on our four hours of sleep.

Ghosts may not exist but I definitely saw zombies in the forest

Nah . . . That's the Forest Clubbers on four hours' sleep

Oh.

Does she get up this early every day? Must be an army thing.

We all assemble with bed-head hair and half-closed eyelids (very un-

Meanwhile, back in the barracks . . .

OK . . . 2 a.m., troops! Up you get!

Chop chop!

army). We're wearing our swimwear under our civvies (a very army term for normal clothes). We yawn and rub our eyes (also very un-army) as we get ready to pile into the minibus.

'No need for the minibus,' declares Edmonds.
'We'll go on foot.'

Great! Just as I thought! A five-hundred-mile
hike to the nearest pool and then we'll
probably have to swim a thousand
lengths! And all of this on just FOUR
HOURS' SLEEP!

But, in fact, we walk for all of two minutes
before Edmonds barks, 'Get changed! Quick smart!
Nothing like an early morning dip!'

No way!!

We're going swimming

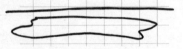

IN THE LAKE?! It'll be freezing with a capital F. F
Factor? Freezing Factor, more like! We all look at
her as though she's completely lost the plot.

'I'll go first!' she
cries, throwing off her
army coat and taking a
running jump straight
into the lake.

No. Way. The lake has vapour coming off it, making it look really hot and steamy, but we know only too well that it isn't steam, it's actually water vapour condensing when it hits the cold air.

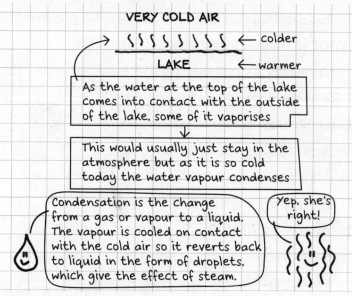

VERY COLD AIR

← colder

LAKE ← warmer

As the water at the top of the lake comes into contact with the outside of the lake, some of it vaporises

This would usually just stay in the atmosphere but as it is so cold today the water vapour condenses

Condensation is the change from a gas or vapour to a liquid. The vapour is cooled on contact with the cold air so it reverts back to liquid in the form of droplets, which give the effect of steam.

Yep, she's right!

Brrrrrr! Just thinking about it makes me feel cold.

'Come on then!' urges Edmonds. 'It's glorious in here!'

'Geronimo!!!!' cries Axel, launching himself into the lake at full pelt.

yee ha!

We're all in our swimming costumes by now and the goosebumps have kicked in. The quicker we're in the water and swimming about to warm up, the better.

'Go on, Alison! You next!' taunts Suzie. 'You know you want to!!'

'You can do it, Alison!' Axel joins in, cheering on  his new friend and making FULL eye contact.

In she goes!

Wonders  will never cease! Not to be outdone by Alison, Suzie follows suit.

And not to be outdone by Suzie, Jake divebombs 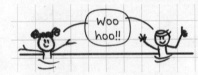 in straight after, grabbing Keziah and pulling her in with him.

It's like a chain reaction. Kind of like watching dominoes topple over.

Now there's only one person left . . . me. GREAT.

The water looks so unappealing. Do I have to go in? The others are splashing about furiously to warm up and seem to be having loads of fun.

'Come on, Cookie!' shouts Edmonds. 'We're going to get rid of all this floating rubbish, carrying on your good work from yesterday! Let's save the planet!'

200

There's no avoiding it. I have to go in. My FOMO coupled with the fact that I don't have much choice in the matter forces my legs into action. My brain makes me run towards the water, despite the rest of my body resisting.

SPLASH!!!

In I go. It's like my whole head is instantaneously frozen. On top of feeling like I'm now inside a block of solid ice, water has gone up my nose and it's causing a horrible stinging sensation. I begin swimming about frantically to warm myself up. My body is all cold and tingly. I make my way towards an empty water bottle bobbing on the surface. Me and Axel grab it at the same time . . .

'Mine!' I say, trying to yank it off him as if we're in a tug of war.

Suddenly we all start to get a bit competitive. We swim around excitedly, each trying to grab the most pieces of plastic pollution. At one point, me and Jake both reach for the same polythene bag and it splits. 'Half each,' he says with a twinkle in his eye.

Was that twinkle for me? Am I forgiven? He swims off and I feel that maybe everything's going to be OK between us again.

'This would make quite a good Olympic sport,' says Edmonds.

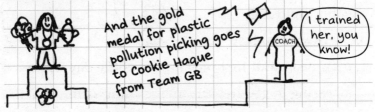

'And it would save the planet in the process,' she continues, laughing to herself as if she's cracked a great joke.

We do a really good job of clearing the lake.

When we finally come out of the water, we're all absolutely freezing. Thankfully there are hot showers in the shed-like building at the lake's edge. Warmth again. Sheer bliss! I dry off and we have breakfast around the campfire. Suzie has brought about thirty different shower gels and shampoos with her. She takes so long in the shower while crooning away to Aliana Tiny that I manage to eat my entire breakfast while she's still in there scrubbing behind her ears. The campfire hash that

Mrs Edmonds has made us is SO yummy and, better still, Suzie is oblivious that I've eaten anything.

Yum!! Eating in daylight is so good. Nocturnal animals don't know what they're missing!

Daylight is so overrated!

After breakfast, it's time for our first big activity of the day. We're all raring to go after our invigorating swim, which has more than woken us up. We're all dressed in our outdoor gear, ready for business. Axel has even painted war stripes on his face again and he's

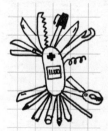

brought along his chunky super-duper Swiss Army knife, which has all sorts of cool bits and pieces tucked away inside it. We're prepared for anything.

After a short walk through the woods, we stop by a giant zipwire, suspended high in the tree canopy.

Some other kids have just finished it and are walking off in good spirits.

'Welcome to the 100-per-cent eco-friendly zipwire!' says Edmonds.

'How can a zipwire be eco-friendly?' asks Axel.

I don't throw any plastic in the sea!

'The special thing about this one is that it's been made purely out of . . . rubbish!' Edmonds replies.

Huh?!!

'All the materials used to make it are recycled,' she explains. 'The wooden frame is made from reclaimed wood, the rubber chippings out of old tyres, and even the rope itself has been made from recycled fibres.'

That is pretty impressive for such a big structure. Looking up, it seems very high.

Suzie and Alison are really excited and begin jumping up and down with glee. They'll be fine with this – they do gymnastics and other sporty activities out of choice.

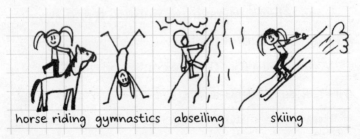

I don't.

We climb up what feels like thousands of steps housed in the big wooden frame, right to the very top of the zipwire where our instructor awaits us.

'Who's first?' he asks.

'Cookie! You were last in the lake, so how about you?' Edmonds chips in helpfully.

How about me? How about no thanks?! How about . . . well . . . I stop and think about it. Maybe I should go first for once? Being last in the lake was pretty embarrassing and how hard could this be? All you have to do is hold on and let gravity do the work. I look at Axel who for once is not staring at the ground but screwing his eyes together tightly, paralysed by his fear of heights. Probably just as well, as the last group of kids look like ants from up here.

Right! I can do this. I'll do it for Axel.

The instructor clips me into a safety harness and makes me grab onto a loop of rope. Everyone counts me down from ten . . .

TEN . . . this rope is really thick . . .

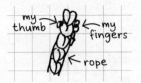 NINE . . . my fingers aren't quite managing to grip it . . .

EIGHT . . . everybody's watching me . . .

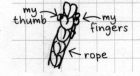 SEVEN . . . do zipwires ever break with people on them?

Thank goodness it's easier than I thought to hold on – that weight lifting paid off!

Oh . . .

SIX . . . This rope really is very thick . . .

 FIVE . . . my fingers really aren't managing to grip it . . .

FOUR . . . I move forward so my toes are over the edge . . .

THREE . . . I flash a fake smile to boost Axel's confidence . . .

TWO . . . his eyes are closed! What a waste!

ONE . . . I really haven't got a good grip . . .

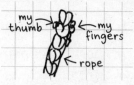

Before I have time to tighten my hands around the rope and shout 'I'm not ready!' the instructor pushes me off the edge . . .

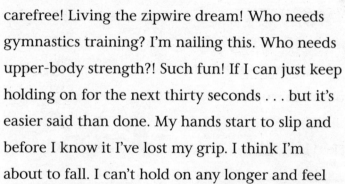

Wheeeeeeeeeeeeee!

I'm zipping through the air like Tarzan. Wind in my hair, carefree! Living the zipwire dream! Who needs gymnastics training? I'm nailing this. Who needs upper-body strength?! Such fun! If I can just keep holding on for the next thirty seconds . . . but it's easier said than done. My hands start to slip and before I know it I've lost my grip. I think I'm about to fall. I can't hold on any longer and feel myself letting go . . .

Going, going, gone . . .

WAAAAH!!!

I've fallen! I'm dangling from the zipwire like a rag doll in a safety harness. I stumble over at the bottom and fall face-first into the wet mud.

It's a bit like being in a bog. Before I have time to properly unclip myself and manoeuvre out of the way, Suzie comes hurtling towards me. Splat! She lands right on top of me.

We panic, shuffling to one side on our bums in the sticky, thick gloop trying to clear the way for Alison.

Alison manages to finish on her feet, which really annoys Suzie. This is made worse by the fact that she bursts out laughing at the sight of the two of us caked in mud.

Suzie, who is already fuming because she's covered in 'bacteria', hurls some mud at Alison. It lands slap bang in the middle of her face.

Before I know it, the others start to join us one by one down the zipwire, oblivious as to what's going on until they land and get caught up in the crossfire.

We all end up hurling mud at each

other like there's no tomorrow. It's so much fun.

Mud is flying in every direction – I'm covered in the stuff. Even Jake splats me on the head, which could be a sign that he's forgiven me – I'm not sure.

Then Axel runs in from the side, jumping on top of us all as though we're in a rugby scrum.

He's chickened out of doing the zipwire and walked back down the steps! So much for me leading the way to help him conquer his fear of heights. Oh well . . . he seems to be loving every minute of our mud festival!

MUD FESTIVAL
. . . better than Glastonbury . . .
ACTS INCLUDE
• MUD FIGHT
• DJ EDMONDS
• THE MARSHMALLOW MONSTER
* BOOK NOW TO AVOID DISAPPOINTMENT!! *

Meanwhile, it's like something primal has awoken inside of us and we all start painting war stripes on our faces with mud, except for Suzie who has crawled out of the bog and is standing there screaming at the top of her lungs.

Being in the thick, warm mud is actually quite comforting, I guess in the same way that people might pay for it as an expensive spa treatment.

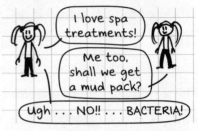

Once again, we're all loving our Forest Club experience!

Just then a voice booms out from behind us, 'INCOMING!!!' Edmonds has launched herself down the zipwire and is hurtling towards us like a herd of elephants.

Oh no! We're bound to be in for it when she sees what we're up to . . .

'FORESTERS, PLEASE!!' she yells. 'Where are your

manners?! No mud bathing without me!' And with that, she joins in!!!

CHAPTER 18

Moral Compass

After having so much fun, it's a bit of a comedown when I get back to our tent from the shower. I'm freezing cold, and my hair

is soaking wet and clinging to my face. My fingers are like prunes.

Worse still, I'm now deaf in one ear.

During our swamp antics, Jake flung a load of mud at me, which went all over the side of my face. It hit me slap-bang on my right ear, partly blocking it.

1. Cookie, do you want to hear a secret? I'll whisper it to you . . .
2. This will be good — I love secrets
3. Oh . . . I can't hear in that ear
4. Good secret!
Thank goodness for two ears!

At the time, I hadn't thought much of it, as the rest

of me was also caked in mud, but in the shower, I tried to wash the mud out and now somehow my whole ear is blocked.

Is it mud? Is it water? A combination of the two? More importantly, will it ever unblock itself? Will I be able to hear properly again? Will I be able to use my old headphones that are broken in one ear?

Shivering, I trudge back to the campfire with Suzie to hear all about what our next ordeal (I mean, activity) would be. At least the fire is warm. I sit huddling by it, sticking my hands out towards the heat like a poor person in Victorian times. I'm really feeling sorry for myself.

BASIC HUMAN NEEDS

Surely warmth is one of our fundamental basic human rights, along with shelter, food, water and clothing?

Edmonds' foghorn of a voice interrupts my thoughts.

'For our next challenge, I'm going to split the boys up. Axel – you can join Cookie and Suzie.

Jake – you can join the other team.'

Great. We're like a couple now just because we're sharing a tent! 'CookieandSuzie'. Ugh!

She says it like it's one word. It just doesn't have the same ring as 'CookieandKeziah'. Now *that* sounds cool. I'm expecting Alison to be annoyed that she's not with Suzie but she doesn't seem that fussed. What does she know that I don't? Is it the bacteria challenge next?!

First team to not mind if they break a nail are the winners!

'Listen up, teams!' barks Edmonds. 'After lunch, you will be . . . orienteering.'

Edmonds explains that we'll have to use a map and a compass to find big yellow stars that have eco-facts on

Orienteering?!

Is that something to do with the Orient?

them. She's hidden them around the forest and once we've collected them all, we'll have to find our way back to the campsite. The other team are excited about this activity. I would be too if I was on their team. But right now, all I have are visions of Suzie

...to take the lead and ...etting us lost by holding the map upside down . . .

OK, guys! Straight on, then left. Easy

The needle is pointing E so we must be going west

. . . or something equally annoying.

Imagine getting lost here at night with Suzie. We'd have to scavenge for worms and grubs to stay alive!

Please don't eat me!

What if we become feral and have to live in the forest forever?

I found some edible mushrooms

Yay!

I'm not eating that — it may have bacteria

But we're starving to death!

After lunch, our two teams assemble in their tents to get ready for the challenge ahead. My ear is still playing up.

'I'm sure Jake flung that mud at you on purpose,' says Suzie. 'So irresponsible of him. All that dirt and bacteria! You might get an ear infection. You could even lose your hearing! I saw a thing on telly once where someone got a tiny spot while they were out in the wilderness. It got infected and the infection grew and grew and grew until they had to have their leg amputated.'

> Oops, sorry, don't blame me, I'm just a spot!

Thanks for that, Suzie! Feeling really good about my ear now!

Suzie opens her giant hot-pink cosmetics bag and pulls out a cotton bud. 'Here! Clear your ear out with this!' she says, passing it over.

'You're not supposed to use those, Suzie!' I reply. 'They can make it worse and even perforate your ear drum!'

'I've got a directional slimline-beam high-intensity torch on here,' says Axel, pulling out his swanky Swiss Army knife and shining the light in my ear. Suzie peers inside. Aaah! My team are looking after me . . .

'We should play a trick on the others. Revenge is sweet!' says Suzie, screwing up her eyes to get a better look in my ear. 'It would be soooooo funny!'

'Err . . .' I reply uncertainly. Huh? I'm not really sure what she's on about.

'Maps are out here in case you want to do any pre-planning, teams,' Edmonds' voice booms from outside. Axel bounds off to get one.

'That's it!' says Suzie. 'We could swap their map for a fake one, then they'd totally get lost!'

'Where are you going to get a fake map from?!' I ask, relieved that this revenge plan would never work in a million years. 'Jake and Keziah aren't dumb! They'll never fall for a fake map!'

'You'd have to do something way smarter than that,' I point out,

Why has someone swapped our map for a copy of Hair and Nails magazine?

'like stick a magnet to their compass so the needle keeps pointing in the wrong direction.'

Suzie's eyes light up and I instantly regret this suggestion. I'd only been trying to highlight how bad her map idea was . . . not give her a workable plan! Oh well. She'll never find a magnet in the middle of a forest.

We don't tend to hang out in forests!

'But where will we get a magnet in the middle of a forest?' says Suzie.

'There'll be one in your speaker,' chimes in Axel. He's just re-entered the tent clutching a map with 'Red Team' written on it in marker pen. Poor Axel is oblivious to the fact that he's now helping Suzie with her conniving scheme.

He has no idea

Suzie wastes no time trying to find a screwdriver on Axel's pocket knife so she can take her brand-new Bluetooth speaker apart. Is she crazy?! What a waste of money! She only just got that speaker!

No, don't unscrew me, are you crazy? All for a silly prank!

'That contains an electromagnet,' I say, thinking on my feet. 'It needs electricity to work. Besides, it would be way too big to stick to a compass without the others noticing!'

Compass
Electromagnet (obvious!)

I don't want us to sabotage the orienteering and get my friends lost. Jake might be ignoring me but I know deep down he wouldn't have thrown that mud at me maliciously. There's no need for revenge. Besides, he'll never forgive me if I get him lost in the forest on top of the whole Aliana debacle.

'Yeah, I suppose you're right,' shrugs Suzie,

putting the rest of the cotton buds back into her cosmetics bag. I breathe a sigh of relief.

'Got it!' she yells just as she's about to close the bag. 'The magnet in the clasp of my cosmetics bag! That'll do the trick!'

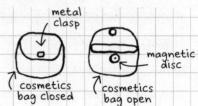

Oh no! How did Suzie work that out? And how on earth has she managed to find a magnet in the middle of a forest?! Where

We do get around, you know, especially us fridge magnets . . . I'm from Brazil!

has this flash of genius come from?! Even I hadn't thought of that!

Suzie begins unscrewing the clasp on the bag as I try to convince her not to.

'Suzie! You'll ruin your bag!' I protest. 'It won't close properly anymore and it's so nice with all its, err . . . unicorns!'

Since when do you like unicorns, Cookie? You don't own anything with a unicorn on it!

'Brilliant excuse to get a new one, Cooks!' she says, flashing me a huge grin.

Oh brother! This magnet is perfect.

magnet

A small round metal disc that's flat enough to stick onto the back of a compass and go unnoticed.

Suzie's delighted, whereas I am far from it. I shoot a look of desperation towards Axel but he's staring at the floor. No surprises there.

Suzie pulls a small bottle of liquid out from inside her cosmetics bag. She looks extremely pleased with herself.

'What's that?' I ask.

'Nail glue!' she says, applying it to the back of the magnet, ready to stick it onto the other team's compass.

Nail glue?! Another flash of genius, where did that come from?!

'Hope you're nearly ready to go, teams,' Edmonds shouts into our tent. 'Your compasses and maps are out here!'

'I'll get ours!' says Suzie, zooming off.

'Yellow Team, you'll go first, leaving at 1400 hours precisely,' yells Edmonds. 'Red Team, you'll follow on at 1410 hours.'

She'd already explained to us earlier that teams

are always staggered in orienteering so they can't copy each other.

This is gobbledygook – let's just follow the other team. This map is RUBBISH!

Suzie returns with our map and compass and tells us she's stuck the magnet onto the other team's compass. Oh no! They'll be lost in no time. The needle of the compass will get confused between the magnet's north pole and the earth's magnetic north pole.

Huh? I'm confused

I don't know where to point!

I'm more worried than I've been all trip, and that's saying something!

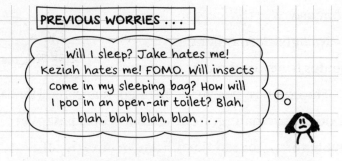

PREVIOUS WORRIES . . .

Will I sleep? Jake hates me! Keziah hates me! FOMO. Will insects come in my sleeping bag? How will I poo in an open-air toilet? Blah, blah, blah, blah, blah . . .

This is a total disaster! I really don't want us to sabotage the other team and I really don't want them to get lost. I just want us all to have fun. That's when I enjoy Forest Club the most – like when we did the scavenger hunt or when we cleared the lake

of all the floating rubbish. This is NOT what I want
AT ALL. I need to let the others know somehow.
Maybe I can get the magnet off their compass
without them noticing or, better still, switch it
with ours.

I grab our compass off Suzie and run out of the
tent before she can say anything. I need to salvage
this situation.

I dash over to where the Yellow
Team have been getting ready . . .
but it's too late. The tent is empty.

The compass has gone. The map has gone. The
Yellow Team have gone. It's two minutes past
two. I've just missed them. They're already off
orienteering and soon they'll be lost. What can I
do? We aren't allowed to leave for another eight
minutes . . .

'Are you alright, Cookie?' barks Edmonds.

'Yes,' I reply. But I'm not. I feel physically sick.

CHAPTER 19

Orienteering

'**Fourteen** hundred and ten hours!' booms Edmonds. 'That's army speak for 2.10 p.m. Off you go!'

I have a sinking feeling in my stomach. My hands are sweating. I've never felt this panicky in my entire life. I can't even look Suzie in the eye – it would just make me angry – so instead I look at the ground like Axel usually does. Only he isn't this time . . . he's in action-mode.

Adventure ready!

For some inexplicable reason, he's wearing a rucksack that's almost larger than him, with lots of bits and pieces hanging off it. It's like a larger, wearable version of his Swiss Army knife! He's scrutinising the map while Suzie is relishing wearing the compass around her neck. She's striding two metres ahead of us as though it gives her some sort of authority. It's like she thinks she's our leader.

I feel like I'm not even with the other two. It's like my brain isn't connected to the rest of my body. I'm numb. I just can't shake the feeling of utter guilt. How could Suzie do something like this and not feel bad about it? Maybe she's a psychopath? Roubi once told me about psychopaths. They're mean people who do mean things and don't feel sorry or guilty about it.

They can often be charming and big-headed, like they think they're special and important! That's Suzie all over. They can't help lying lots either . . . uh oh! I hope I'm not one. Mind you, I don't think I'm special or important, so hopefully that rules me out. Psychopaths often have complex criminal behaviour too. Hmmmm . . . like sticking magnets to compasses? They're also cold and unemotional. Phew . . . I'm pretty emotional, so hopefully I'm safe! Unlike Suzie . . .

How have I ended up as part of 'SuzieandCookie'? This is all a terrible mistake. I had perfectly good friends and now I've probably lost them forever. Lost!!! Aargghhh!!! I'd almost forgotten . . . they probably ARE lost by now in the deepest part of the forest. Keziah will be freaking out about the darkness and Alison will probably be hallucinating ghosts. Meanwhile, Jake will be getting angrier with me by the minute, as they wander around aimlessly with a mad, broken compass.

Uh oh, there must be a ghost in this compass – it's acting possessed!

'You're being very quiet, Cookie,' says Suzie, who's been wittering away with Axel as if nothing is wrong. Psychopath!

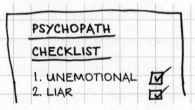

PSYCHOPATH
CHECKLIST
1. UNEMOTIONAL ☑
2. LIAR ☑

You've just got three people lost . . . potentially forever!! And I'm not being quiet – it's very noisy in my brain right now, I'll have you know. It's going into overdrive with worry. It won't stop talking to me!!!

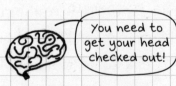

You need to get your head checked out!

Axel won't stop talking to me either. He's obsessed with the map and is poring over every single little detail.

Poor Keziah! Poor Jake!

Poor Alison too!

'How come you're being so quiet?' Suzie persists.

'I just don't feel well,' I lie.
Psychopath?

'Hope your ear isn't still playing up,' she says, winking at me, acting all charming. Psychopath.

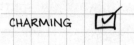

'Poor you!' she says. 'You don't deserve an ear infection!'

'My ear's fine now,' I lie.
Again. Psychopath?

My ear's actually still blocked but I don't want her blaming Jake or being mean about him again. Nice person. Not a psychopath.

'I hope the others aren't too lost,' says Axel, like he's just read my mind.

'Who cares!' says Suzie. No guilt. Psychopath.

LACK OF REMORSE OR GUILT ☑

'I CARE!!!' I yell. And I mean it. Phew! I'm definitely not a psychopath.

DOESN'T CARE ABOUT OTHER PEOPLE ☐

Suzie says nothing but continues to march ahead, wielding her compass in a power-crazed fashion. That girl has delusions of grandeur. She thinks she's more important than she is. Psychopath.

With this compass around my neck I WIELD POWER!

DELUSIONS OF GRANDEUR ☑

'Are we walking due south-east?' asks Axel. 'We need to walk due south-east till we hit a stream.'

'Errrrrr . . . I'm not sure,' says Suzie, who clearly has no idea how to actually use a compass.

'You're holding it upside down!' says Axel, grabbing it off her.

If we can't find a star without a magnet stuck to our compass, who knows what the others are going through right now?!

'The stream!' shouts Axel, pointing to a small

channel of running water. 'There's our first star!'

Suzie rushes over and picks it up. 'Yey!!!' she yells, jumping up and down and hugging Axel.

Weird! Most unlikely combination of two people hugging ever! Axel stiffens up like a robot and looks super awkward.

I wish I could have joined in the celebrations. Usually I'm all for problem-solving and mental challenges but I just can't get enthusiastic right now.

After this, Suzie lets Axel have both the map and the compass and soon we're on fire. We whizz around from point to point finding stars like we do it every day of the week. Axel's a natural at this. When we're halfway through, we sit down on some logs in a clearing and he pulls three cups and a flask of hot chocolate out from his rucksack.

'Where did you get this from?' asks Suzie.

'I made it back at camp,' says Axel.

'Nice one,' I say, glugging back the hot chocolate, which is warm and comforting, and makes me feel a little better.

'I won't get germs off this, will I?' says Suzie.

'The cups are clean and the hot chocolate was made with boiling water, which is safe to drink, I think,' says Axel.

'Most bacteria can't survive at such a high temperature,' I explain.

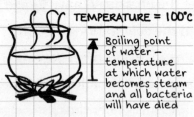

'Safe to drink as long as you don't burn your tongue,' laughs Axel.

'I won't burn my tongue!' says Suzie, blowing on her hot chocolate to cool it down.

'Shame!' I mutter under my breath.

'I heard that!' says Suzie. 'You're acting really weird, Cookie!'

'Why?! Because I'm not a psychopath?!' I shout. 'Because I feel bad about sending three Year-Fivers off into the woods to get lost for who knows how long without the basic needs of food, shelter and

warmth? Yes, Suzie, I'm SO weird. Welcome to the
weird team with me and Axel, the weirdos.'

There's an awkward silence.

'Weird is cool!' says Axel,
trying to diffuse the situation, but it doesn't really
work. Suzie is quiet for the rest of the challenge, as

am I, which means
Axel has to do most
of the chatting. Talk
about role reversal!

Axel navigates us back to camp with ease, having
found all our yellow stars in no time at all.

'Goodness!' remarks Edmonds. 'You managed to
beat the other team back even though they started
first! How impressive!'

'And we stopped for hot
chocolate,' boasts Suzie. Psychopath.

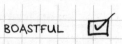

'Wonderful!' says Edmonds. 'The other team will
be so jealous when they get back.'

If they get back. And furious is probably more
accurate.

'How about a piece of Kendal
Mint Cake for each of our
winners?' says Mrs Edmonds.

Winners?! We're saboteurs, not winners! The only reason that we're back first is that the other team are LOST! Potentially FOREVER! And it's ALL MY FAULT for giving Suzie my excellent science advice. If only I'd kept my big mouth shut then none of this would ever have happened.

I feel too sick to eat. It's not like me to turn down cake. I must feel bad. Plus, I've never even tried Kendal Mint Cake before and I still don't want any. Axel gobbles his down and Suzie spits hers out, claiming it tastes like toothpaste. It smells like toothpaste, to be honest. Pretty strong toothpaste.

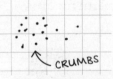

'Looks like it's just me and you, Axel,' chuckles Edmonds as they polish it off between them.

Half an hour passes and Edmonds starts looking at her watch, a little concerned. 'Hmm . . . they should really be back by now . . . the course wasn't too hard . . . and you lot seemed to manage it OK.'

230

It'll be getting dark soon. Poor Keziah. She must be terrified. And Alison will be thinking there's a ghost behind every tree.

Another half an hour passes and Edmonds is now starting to get really worried.

← furrowed brow showing extreme worry

'I'm leaving you this phone,' she barks at us. 'Call the police if I'm not back by quarter to.' Then she disappears off into the forest.

For the next half an hour, I clock-watch as the minutes tick away. Suzie is clearly starting to worry too. Not a psychopath after all?

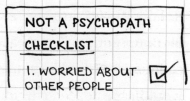

NOT A PSYCHOPATH CHECKLIST

1. WORRIED ABOUT OTHER PEOPLE ☑

It feels as though we're waiting there for hours. If you told me that days had passed, I might have almost believed it. It's getting properly dark. No light except for the moon. No Edmonds. No Yellow Team.

'I think you should make that call,' says Axel, staring at the ground.

Sickened to the core, I begin to dial 9-9-9 into the

phone . . . and at that exact same moment Edmonds re-emerges from the forest followed by none other than Alison, Keziah and Jake. All intact. All alive. Alison and Keziah both look pale, like they've seen a ghost. Jake doesn't look scared. . . just angry.

'Nothing to worry about, Foresters! The Yellow Team must have taken an incorrect turn and ended up on the wrong path. All good now though. There's soup and rolls back at camp and then time for an early night, I reckon.'

As the others trudge back towards their tents, Jake walks over to me and hands me the magnet. 'I think this is yours', he says, looking angrier and more upset than I've ever seen him before. 'Suzie's too stupid to think of something like this . . . and it wouldn't cross Axel's mind. I know it was you,' he snarls.

And with that, he walks away, leaving me feeling the worst I've ever felt in my entire life.

CHAPTER 20

Facing Fear in the Face

So now EVERYONE is cross with me. Great.

Jake thinks I stuck the magnet to the compass. Alison thinks I've stolen her best friend. Suzie and I aren't speaking anyway. And as for Axel, well, he just looks at the ground most of the time so who knows what's going on in his head?! But worst of all, Keziah, who never gets cross at anyone, looks really hurt and angry. Well, as angry as Keziah can ever look.

← Keziah's angry face!

Things aren't good.

Keziah must know I would never have stuck that magnet to the compass, but Jake certainly thinks I did. I'm not sure if he's told Alison, but you can bet he's been bad-mouthing me to Keziah.

Surely deep down she's unsure whether I did it or not?! I really hope so. She knows I'm not a bad person. This is all SO unfair. I haven't done anything wrong. It was 'Psychopath Suzie'. Only I don't think she actually is a psychopath.

To be fair she looked really guilty and apologetic after Edmonds had gone into the forest. She knows she's been totally irresponsible.

That night, me and Suzie go to sleep without speaking a word to each other.

I can tell she's awake from her breathing though. Yep, I can actually recognise the breathing sounds and

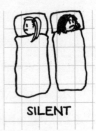

rhythm of Suzie when she's sleeping now – we really are becoming a couple! Help!!

Through my unblocked ear I'm sure I can hear sniffing and the faint sound of muffled crying. I actually feel a bit sorry for her.

The next morning, my ear is back to normal just in time for our final activity: an army-style assault course. I'm really not in the mood for this.

Edmonds explains that it's a group challenge and that it'll be daunting in parts, so we'll all need to work together to beat the clock. Great . . . half of us aren't even speaking to each other, so this is the PERFECT time for a teamwork exercise . . . NOT!

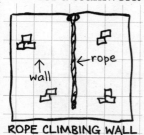

ROPE CLIMBING WALL

Our first obstacle is a really high climbing wall.

We all clamber over it without saying a word to one another. There is zero teamwork involved. Quiet, angry, yet determined, we tackle the wall as though we're stealth-like ninjas: deadly silent with faces like thunder. Until Suzie stumbles into the mud on the other side, that is, and a shrill scream punctures the silence.

She blames Jake for shoving into her, who then blames me, but I reckon it's Alison's fault. We all end up arguing over it, including 'non-confrontational'

Keziah . . . but our yells are interrupted by a shriek of delight.

'I did it!' cries Axel, catching up with us all and punching the sky. 'At last! I've conquered my fear!'

We hadn't noticed that Axel hadn't made it over the wall up until now as we'd been too busy arguing. We all feel guilty (not psychopaths) that we didn't help him over but he insists that we *did* help by ignoring him and squabbling amongst ourselves!!! Apparently, he found it much easier to climb over without anyone looking at him! Hurray for teamwork, I guess?!

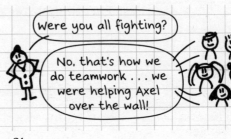

Next, we come across an extremely dark tunnel that we have to crawl along.

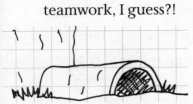

It's a tight squeeze and pretty tricky to manoeuvre through but we all manage in the end – except for Keziah. How typical that now would be the exact moment that the batteries run out in her torch, paralysing her with fear. We all try to encourage her through the tunnel's pitch-black interior.

It's no use though, she's completely distraught. I know what I have to do. In a superhero-like move and a bid to regain her friendship, I head straight back into the tunnel. When I reach her, I grab onto her hand and hold it tightly, guiding her out with me and reassuring her the whole way. As she's a captive audience, I also take the opportunity to explain to her that the magnet incident was nothing to do with me.

I feel great to be reunited with KK as she clutches onto my hand. BFFs!

'I did it! I've conquered my fear too!' cries Keziah, punching the sky as we come out into the light just like Axel did moments before. We all laugh and Axel leaps into the air, overcome with excitement.

He gives Keziah a huge
hug. SO un-Axel! We
all join in.

Two tasks down, three to go. This is getting
exciting. It isn't easy but somehow we're storming

through this
assault course
and having fun
together like a proper team.

As we near the next stage of the course, Suzie
comes over to me. 'You know that was so amazing
when you went back for Keziah,' she says, 'it really
was.' She smiles and it's a totally genuine
smile and I know she means it.

'I couldn't have left her,' I say, smiling back. 'She'd
have done the same for me. I guess that's what best

friends are for.' As I'm
saying it, I can tell
that Suzie is really
taking in my words.

Oh help!! Next up is a mud pit (or bacteria pit as
Suzie would call it).

MUD PIT

She'll never get through this. She was bad enough at the bottom of the zipwire, and that was mild in comparison. We all begin squelching our way across it, except for Suzie, who's refusing to budge. She just stands there squealing at the side.

ARGHH!!

BACTERIA!!

It's like wading through dense, brown treacle. It's right up to our thighs and it's so thick that it takes a lot of body strength to actually move through it. Then, around the mid-way point, Alison gets stuck and starts screaming.

'I can't move,' she wails. 'My foot is trapped, I'll never get out!'

From where we are, it would be almost impossible to pull her out. Without hesitation or a second thought, in rushes Suzie. It's as if she's replicating my superhero rescue mission in a bid to make up with Alison. Alison is so touched by Suzie saving her that she actually cries tears of joy. She's beside herself with happiness. It practically has me welling up too.

How come you're so happy?

I'm a happy tear

'Thanks so much, Suze,' sniffs Alison.

'It's what best friends are for,' says Suzie, squeezing her arm.

Wonder where you got that phrase from, 'Suze'?!

Our last challenge is to crawl under a scramble net and then find our way through a cave . . .

haunted cave

scramble net

. . . which, according to Edmonds, the locals think is haunted. Apparently, someone once went missing in it only to reappear a few days later with complete memory loss!!

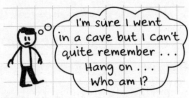

But let's face it, that story's totally made up to stop kids hanging about in it, if you ask me. It doesn't seem to faze Alison in the slightest though. With her new-found euphoria at making up with Suzie, she's through it in no time at all. She's focused and determined as if her fear of ghosts was never even a thing!

Fears and obstacles conquered, all that remains is a short cross-country run through a field to the finish line.

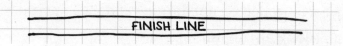

FINISH LINE

Job done. Mission complete. Stop the clock!

As we make our way across the field, it's plain to see that it's strewn with rubbish. I stop in my tracks as I realise something.

'Hey, guys . . . all the other activities have had an environmental twist . . . I reckon this is a test!'

ACTIVITY	ENVIRONMENTAL SPIN
ZIPWIRE	This was 100% recycled
ORIENTEERING	We had to find eco facts on stars
LAKE SWIM	We cleared the plastic pollution from the lake

At the start of the trip, we'd been given an essentials kit full of stuff like plasters, a small pen and notepad, and other items including a bin bag!! Now I think I know why . . .

'Yeah, you're right!' agrees Keziah. 'This must be a test! There was a whole thing about taking care of the countryside in the handouts. There was even a massive section on not littering and the importance of picking up rubbish.'

'*And* she was talking about keeping the countryside clean in her pep talk before  we came camping,' adds Jake. 'Come to think of it, she mentioned it on the way here.'

JAKE IS AGREEING WITH ME!!!! He wasn't talking to me but he was acknowledging something I'd said. There's hope!

Immediately, we all set about picking up the bits of rubbish that are strewn across the field.

It's like Suzie and Alison have never been apart. They're laughing and joking together as they pick up bits of litter without even caring about germs and bacteria. Now I'm the one feeling jealous of Alison. They have way more in common than me and Suzie ever did! Keziah and Axel are off in the distance having their own competition to see who can pick up more rubbish, so this would be the perfect opportunity to corner Jake.

Plucking up even more courage than I mustered in the tunnel, on the high wall and in the cave put together, I tell Jake everything . . . about selling the Aliana ticket, my unexpected shopping trip and NOT putting the magnet on the compass.

I explain to Jake that my only crime was excellent scientific knowledge – knowing that compasses are magnetic – and surely scientific knowledge should be celebrated, not vilified.

science, technology, engineering and maths

At school we had an assembly on the importance of female scientists and the lack of them in STEM subjects, so you could say I did a good thing.

I pause as I try to fit an unwieldy plastic carton into my binbag. For a moment, Jake is silent. He's stunned, taking it all in . . . then he bursts out laughing.

'Have you quite finished?!!' he says. 'I'm seriously amazed how you managed to keep breathing throughout all of that!'

Yay! Jake's speaking to me. Finally! I'm so relieved. I start welling up again! Wow! This assault course has emotional depths!!

This picking up rubbish is so touching

I explain to Jake that I was upset that he thought Suzie would only be my friend so she could get her hands on the Aliana ticket. I also admit he kind of had a point, but only because I have much less in common with Suzie than with him and Keziah.

'Exactly,' he says, 'and she has more in common with Alison!'

I get it now.

Suzie has more in common with Alison and nothing in common with me. She was only being my friend for the Aliana ticket!

LIGHTBULB MOMENT

Next it's Jake's turn to say sorry. He says he should've known that I wouldn't pull a stunt like the magnet one, but he's just been so preoccupied lately.

Preoccupied with what? Is it something to do with me? Or something else entirely?

Hmm . . . I wonder if everyone knows how to make their farts silent . . .

He says he's tried to tell me a few times but he just hasn't found the right moment. He admits that he now knows what his greatest fear is . . . his parents getting a divorce.

He has tears in his eyes. It all falls into place. Why he's been so distant, why he's been avoiding going home, the suitcases in his parents' bedroom – they weren't for a trip to Disneyland but for his dad moving out of the family home. I put my arms around him and he cries quietly into my jacket.

sniff

Poor Jake

I tell him that parents split up all the time these days and it's often better that way. If they're happier then he'll be happier. Plus, he'll get two homes, two bedrooms, two wardrobes, two lots of toys and maybe even two sets of pocket money! He laughs, all snotty and teary.

It's high time for me to get over my FOMO, so I tell him that he's welcome to have my Aliana ticket if he can bear to go with Suzie!

'Are you kidding?!' he cries. 'Amazing?!! I can totally bear to go with anyone who'll sing all the lyrics and do all the dance moves with me. In fact, I'd LOVE TO!'

All fears conquered and all rubbish collected, it's time to cross the finish line!!!

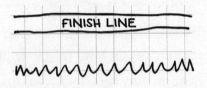

FINISH LINE

CHAPTER 21

Home Sweet Home

We gather round the fire one last time while Edmonds congratulates us all on our wonderful achievement. We'd completed the mission and passed the final test – not to ignore the litter. She hands us each a brown paper goody bag with a certificate, medal, pen, notepad and an 'I Zipwired to Success' badge in it. Tucked away at the bottom there are also lots of leaflets, most of which are adverts, offers and coupons for various outdoorsy stuff like eco-products and camping shops.

We proudly put our medals on.

'You know what?' grins Edmonds. 'You've all helped me get over *my* fear . . . of children.'

I think she's joking at first but she goes on to say that she never knew how to act around kids before us, other than just being plain strict. She saw so much spirit and character in our group during our detention that she hoped we would all sign up for the F Factor. And we did!

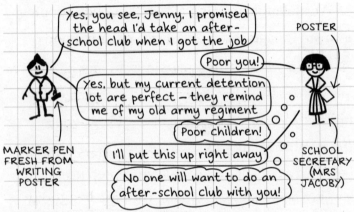

She explains that as she's a supply teacher covering someone who's away, she'll be leaving the school in a couple of weeks' time, so she's incredibly grateful to us. Our pleasure . . . I think?! Although we haven't really done anything apart from just be ourselves! Shame she's going – we all really like her now.

On the way back home, I sit with Keziah in the minibus. Edmonds switches the radio on only for Aliana to come blaring out of the speakers. Oh no! Not again! Suzie and Jake instantly feel the need to

start doing the dance moves in their seats and lip-synching to the whole thing.

We all laugh and sing along, Edmonds bopping away in time as she drives. Everyone's in good spirits. This is the complete OPPOSITE of the journey there.

BEFORE   AFTER

UTTER SILENCE   PARTY BUS!

'Hey!' says Keziah, looking through her goody bag. 'There's a five-pound-off voucher for Mike's Bikes in here. You can put it towards getting a new bike, Cookie!'

Bike = £100		
money collected = so far	£25	voucher
	£5	lunch money
	£5	voucher from Keziah
	£35	total
still needed		
£100 − £35 = £65		

'You can have mine if you like!' says Suzie UNPROMPTED, waving her voucher in the air. 'I'll never buy a bike there before this expires at the end of the month! Plus, I just got a brand-new unicorn bike last week!' Wonders will never cease!

> Bike = £100
>
> money collected = so far
> £25 voucher
> £5 lunch money
> £5 vouchers from Keziah
> £5 and Suzie
> ___
> £40 total
>
> still needed
> £100 − £40 = £60

The others offer me their vouchers too and before I know it I have thirty pounds' worth of them! I'm sixty pounds of the way to that hundred-pound bike I've seen! I've doubled the amount I had in one bus journey! AMAZING!

> Bike = £100
>
> money collected = so far
> £25 voucher
> £5 lunch money
> £5 vouchers from Keziah
> £5 and Suzie
> £20 4 x other vouchers
> ___
> £60 total
>
> still needed
> £100 − £60 = £40

Forest camp has given me more towards my bike than MY OWN PARENTS! On reflection, the whole thing has been such fun and a really good learning experience.

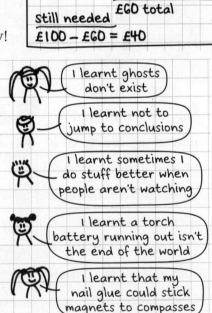

I learnt ghosts don't exist

I learnt not to jump to conclusions

I learnt sometimes I do stuff better when people aren't watching

I learnt a torch battery running out isn't the end of the world

I learnt that my nail glue could stick magnets to compasses

When we finally arrive at the school car park, everyone's parents cheer us off the bus. We greet them with huge hugs and excited chatter. Jake's dad has come to pick him up, which gives Jake the biggest grin I've seen on his face in weeks.

Suzie's parents are amused to see her with unwashed hands. A first!

grubby hands

They joke about it with Alison's parents, who are chuffed that Alison is now actually *looking forward* to going to her great-aunt's 'haunted' mansion.

Ich liebe den Waldclub

Axel and his mum are speaking excitedly at a million miles per hour in German . . .

. . . and Keziah pins her 'I Zipwired to Success' badge onto her dad's newly grown beard.

Errr . . . thanks! I always wanted a badge pinned on my beard! . . . NOT!

'Me and Axel shouldn't have got that badge,' I say. 'After all, I fell off and he didn't even do the zipwire!'

I notice Suzie sidling over to Jake and wonder what's going on. . .

I know, I'll sidle over

No one will notice

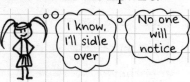

251

'She's probably apologising to him about the whole magnet incident,' says Keziah, reading my mind. 'She's already apologised to me.'

'She's changed!' I laugh.

Jake bounds over to us.

'Hey! Guess what?!' he says.

BEFORE   AFTER

'Suzie said sorry?' I reply.

'Yes,' he continues, 'but also, Alison's parents have just invited Suzie to her great-aunt's stately home the weekend of the Aliana gig, which means she doesn't want her ticket anymore, so you can come with me if you want, Cookie?!'

Errr . . . between Suzie's Bluetooth speaker and the sing-along in the coach, I was pretty sure that if I never heard 'Be Who You Am' again in my life it would be too soon!

I think it's quite catchy actually

'You know what, Jake,' I say, 'you should really go with your dad. It'd be great for you two to have some quality time together.'

Jake's eyes light up. 'Really? That'd be SO amazing! Only if you're sure though.'

'I'm 100 per cent sure,' I reply. He runs off to tell his dad. To be honest, I'm a bit relieved. I've finally got over my fear of missing out! No more FOMO for me!

Jake's dad insists on buying the ticket off Suzie for twenty-five pounds – the same amount that she paid me for it – so it all works out perfectly!

Suzie comes over to me next . . .

'Cookie, I just wanted to say I really am sorry about the whole compass thing. I know you probably think it was mean of me but sometimes I get a bit carried away. I really, really am sorry. I hope you believe me.'

Wow. An apology from Suzie Ashby, and a heartfelt one at that. This seems like a good time for me to fess up too.

'I owe you an apology as well,' I say. 'I totally lied to you about the whole fasting thing. Ramadan was actually in May, but I felt bad that your mum had made all that food and I couldn't eat any of it because it was pork and I'm Muslim! Once I started lying, I found it really hard to own up.'

'No way!' says Suzie, a little taken aback.

'It's true!' I reply. 'I've had to hide from you any time I was eating during the day ever since I was at your house!'

Suzie goes quiet . . . and then bursts out laughing! It does seem totally ridiculous on reflection. I burst out laughing too.

After we've calmed down from our fit of hysterics, she says she also wants to say thank you. She explains that hanging out with me has made her see that she's been taking Alison for granted. She says she's realised how important it is to be there for your friends, which is why she's decided to go and support Alison at her great-aunt's place, just in case ghosts do exist . . .

. . . which they don't. Even Alison doesn't believe in them anymore.

'She'll really appreciate that,' I say. 'It'll mean an awful lot that you're missing the Aliana gig for her.'

'Yeah! And her great-aunt's place is a mansion,' she says excitedly. 'I reckon it's got a pool, stables, tennis courts and everything!' She runs off.

'She's changed!' grins Keziah. 'But not that much!'

'She reminds me of me when I was about to go to her house!' I laugh. Then in my best Suzie voice I say, 'I reckon it's got a pool, stables, tennis courts and everything!'

We both laugh. But we know Suzie has changed a little. I hope it lasts. She seems much more genuine now. I think we've all changed in some way after our camping trip. Changed for the better.

The next week at school whizzes past and thankfully me, Keziah and Jake are totally back to

normal. All us Foresters are
on a post-camping-trip high.

On Friday, Keziah and
Jake suggest we hang out at
the park on the way home from school. As we're
walking out of the school gates, we bump into none
other than Mrs Edmonds.

'Well, hello there, Foresters!' she booms. 'I'm glad
I bumped into you. Next week's my last week so if
I don't catch you before I go, I just wanted to say
how much I enjoyed our wonderful camping trip!!
Thank you!!'

We tell her we should be thanking her and ask
her where she's off to.

She says she's been giving it a lot of thought
and our trip has inspired her to set up some sort of

nationwide environmental-awareness-
themed Forest Club. She wants it to be
a charitable organisation that would
be both fun AND help save the planet
in the process! Good on Edmonds!

'The planet won't save itself!' she says, waving
goodbye as she disappears off. It sounds like a great
idea! We'll all really miss her, but it's good to know

that once she's up and running we can repeat our fabulous adventure again whenever we want!

When we get to the park, it's starting to get pretty windy. Without even thinking about it, the three of us begin collecting up all the loose bits of rubbish that are tumbling around everywhere. We've changed!

'So . . .' says Keziah as we all sit down on a nearby bench. 'Now that you and Jake are on speaking terms again, we thought we would finally give you your birthday present!'

Jake hands me an envelope with a card inside that reads 'Help Save the Planet: ride bikes, not cars!'

'We thought the card was funny,' he says, 'as it doesn't even make sense! You can't ride a car!'

We all giggle.

I open it up and inside is a fifteen-pound voucher for Mike's Bikes. Amazing!

I hug them both. 'Thanks so much, guys! Soon

I'll be able to ride round to Keziah's at weekends! You won't be able to get rid of me!'

Not sure about this whole joined at the hip thing!

My bike is actually within reach now, although it'll probably take me a year to save up the remaining twenty-five pounds. . .

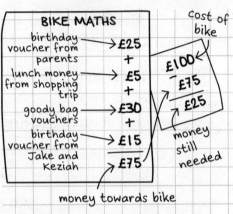

BIKE MATHS

birthday voucher from parents → £25

+

lunch money from shopping trip → £5

+

goody bag vouchers → £30

+

birthday voucher from Jake and Keziah → £15

→ £75

money towards bike

cost of bike

£100

£75

£25

money still needed

But hey . . . a year is better than three years and it'll be worth it in the end!

Jake is going to his dad's new place this evening, so he heads home the same way as Keziah. He's actually really upbeat about it now and is excited to check out his new bedroom.

Maybe my new bedroom will have a ping-pong table!

Good on him. I decide to walk home past the bike shop so I can have a look at my dream bike in the window. But when I get there . . . there's a sign outside. It reads 'Sale on Now!!'

There's a big banner below it that says '25% off all bikes! This week only! Sale Ends Friday!'

25% OFF ALL BIKES! This week only. Sale ends FRIDAY

Huh?!!? It is Friday! This is the last day of the sale! And 25 per cent off one hundred pounds is . . . seventy-five pounds! That's the exact amount I have!!

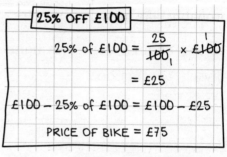

25% OFF £100

$$25\% \text{ of } £100 = \frac{25}{100} \times £100$$

$$= £25$$

$$£100 - 25\% \text{ of } £100 = £100 - £25$$

$$\text{PRICE OF BIKE} = £75$$

My heart starts racing. Without pausing for thought, I rush into the shop and buy the bike there and then, on the spot. It feels impulsive and it feels good. Very good.

Better still, the bike I choose comes with a matching helmet. It looks really cool. I feel so proud riding home on my brand-new bike. I'm so happy. Happy in my own skin just being plain me! Not pretending to fast, not pretending to be best friends with Suzie, not pretending to be into Aliana.

259

I start humming out of pure happiness.

The tune is stuck in my head – it's annoyingly catchy. I hum it all the way home, beaming to myself. Life is good.

APPENDIX

HOW TO MAKE A DAISY CHAIN, COOKIE-STYLE!

Daisy chains have been made since the beginning of time! Well, err, since the beginning of daises, I guess. Jake says that even his great-grandma used to make them. She lived in the countryside and the family still have a book from when she was young and used to press flowers from her back garden. Flower pressing is when you take a flower – the prettier and more colourful the better – and flatten it in a book till it completely dries out and is as thin as paper. Jake said that one time his brother got a Spotter's Guide to Flowers and managed to identify all of the species in his great-grandma's book.

Look, everyone – Great Granny pressed a bellis perennis

What? You mean a daisy?

Materials

As many daisies as you need for your chain!

daisy

You can use all sorts of different wild flowers if you want to vary it up, but daisies and buttercups are ideal as they're the right size. Obviously don't go too crazy picking wild flowers, but the odd few won't hurt.

And certainly don't pick them from other people's gardens!

Yeah, we're living things too, remember!

Can you find any of these wild flowers in the great outdoors? Different flowers come out at different times of the year so don't worry if you don't find them all!

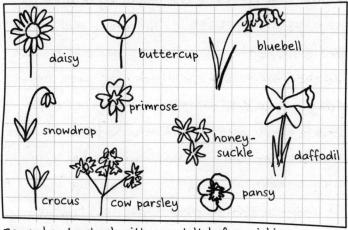

daisy

buttercup

bluebell

primrose

snowdrop

honey-suckle

daffodil

crocus

cow parsley

pansy

Remember to check with an adult before picking flowers out of your garden — you wouldn't want to pull out someone's favourite begonia!

Cookie! Did you pull my begonias out of the garden?

Oops, that was me — happy Valentine's Day!

Method

Pick some daisies from your garden by pulling each wild flower up from the base of the stem. Hold it carefully or all its petals will come off!

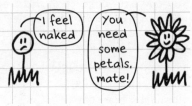

Using your fingernail, score a slit in the stem. Make sure that the slit doesn't go all the way to the edge otherwise the stem will break in half!

A slit like this

But not like this

Repeat this with as many daisies as you want for your daisy chain. If you're making a necklace, you'll want more than if you're making a bracelet!

And if you're making a ring, you'll just need the one . . . me!

Thread the stem of one daisy

Hi down there!

Hiya!

through the slit of another. Repeat this until you have a long chain.

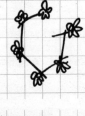

Connect the two ends of your long chain by tying a knot between the two stems.

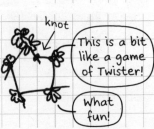

knot

This is a bit like a game of Twister!

What fun!

Wear your chain or give it to a friend. I gave mine to Keziah.

When you've finished wearing your daisy chain you could also press it into a book like Jake's great-grandma used to do with her flowers!

Method for Pressing Flowers

Tape your flowers in between two pages of a notebook.

Put some heavy books (like an encyclopaedia) on top of the notebook to squash the flower.

DICTIONARY
COOKBOOK
THESAURUS
FAIRYTALES

flower is squashed here

Leave the notebook for two to three weeks till the flowers are fully dry! Your dried flowers will look beautiful and will be a lovely keepsake! Jake's great-grandma was from Victorian times and Jake's mum still has the book today!

I wonder if my great-grandson will make daisy chains one day!

Results

Pressing flowers can preserve them for a long time!

Conclusion

When you press something, you squeeze the moisture out of it and therefore stop it from rotting or breaking down naturally. While preserving flowers in this way is fun, what we really need to preserve is our environment. Wouldn't it be awful if we lived in a world where there were no flowers to make daisy chains with? Flowers, and more specifically the trees and plants they belong to, are SO IMPORTANT! Basically, without them we'd all die!

Plants and trees remove carbon dioxide from the air and replace it with oxygen, which is what we breathe.

This process is called photosynthesis and it's how plants make food for themselves to grow.

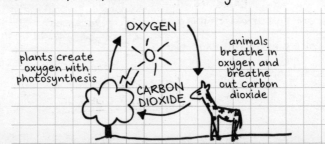

Although it seems like plants are doing absolutely nothing, they're actually working really, really hard.

Stop lying around, grass!

I'm working hard, actually, making oxygen

The oxygen content of our air is determined by the number of plants we have on this planet, which is why it's so important to preserve all our green spaces!

So that's where I went wrong!

And now that us humans create so much carbon dioxide (CO_2) because of modern living, the oxygen content of the air is more vital than ever. The cars we drive, the factories we use, the planes we fly and many other things humans do on a daily basis create carbon emissions.

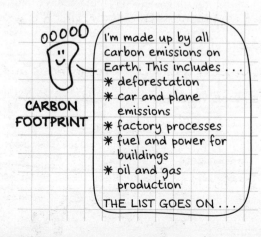

CARBON FOOTPRINT

I'm made up by all carbon emissions on Earth. This includes . . .
* deforestation
* car and plane emissions
* factory processes
* fuel and power for buildings
* oil and gas production

THE LIST GOES ON . . .

Our carbon footprint is destroying the ozone layer!

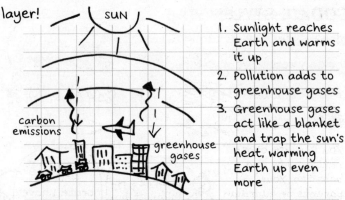

1. Sunlight reaches Earth and warms it up
2. Pollution adds to greenhouse gases
3. Greenhouse gases act like a blanket and trap the sun's heat, warming Earth up even more

We need to reduce our carbon footprint by living more responsibly.

Unlike Suzie Ashby . . .

Huh?

Attic

Bedroom
Turn your light off
Fewer plastic toys

Bathroom
Don't leave the tap running
Showers are better than baths

Kitchen
Don't waste food
Use recyclable packaging

Living room
Don't leave the TV on standby
Turn things off

Don't fill the kettle – just boil what you need

Put pot plants out to generate oxygen

MAKE YOUR OWN MINIBEAST HOTEL, COOKIE-STYLE!

Materials

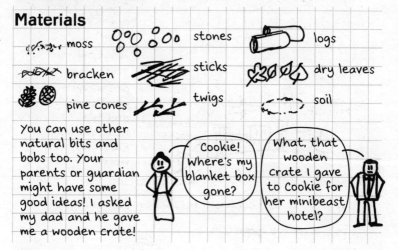

moss

stones

logs

bracken

sticks

dry leaves

pine cones

twigs

soil

You can use other natural bits and bobs too. Your parents or guardian might have some good ideas! I asked my dad and he gave me a wooden crate!

Cookie! Where's my blanket box gone?

What, that wooden crate I gave to Cookie for her minibeast hotel?

Method

First you need to create the base of the hotel by arranging a small pile of logs.

Make sure they're not too big or heavy as you don't want to drop them and hurt yourself!

Ow, get off my foot!

I can't – I've got no legs! I'm a log

If you've got a wooden pallet or a wooden crate like I do then that would make a great base too.

If you can't find anything like that, you could use lots of sticks or a cardboard box instead!

Use me, I'm crate

No you're not, you're an empty cardboard box

Once you've made the basic structure, use all your other materials to fill in the gaps.

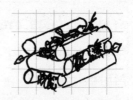

The idea is to provide an environment with loads of nooks, crannies, crevices, tunnels and cosy beds for the minibeasts!

Comfiest bed ever!

Results

Hopefully lots of insects and creatures will come and stay at your hotel! Different insects are attracted to different materials...

MATERIAL	WILDLIFE ATTRACTED
Bark	creepy crawlies e.g. spiders, woodlice
Leaves	ladybirds, as aphids live on leaves (ladybirds eat aphids)
Corrugated cardboard	lacewings
Big holes under and between stones	frogs and toads

Write down in the table on the next page which insects and creatures came to visit your hotel and which bits they stayed in!

Insect	Part of Hotel

Conclusion

Insects love small spaces and dark, cosy atmospheres. Different insects like different environments.

NATURE SCAVENGER HUNT, COOKIE-STYLE!

Materials

A list of the letters
of the alphabet
(I've made you one below!)

Alphabet
list

A pencil

A rubber in case you
make any mistakes!

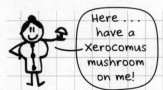

rubber

pencil

Method

Go outside (with your parent or guardian of
course!) and try to find something in nature
beginning with every letter of the alphabet.
Don't expect to get all the letters, as some are
much harder than others, like Q or X. You could
always use reference
books or the Internet to
help you ... Remember,
Mrs Edmonds helped us
out with lots of cheats!

Here ...
have a
Xerocomus
mushroom
on me!

A –

B –

C –

D –

E –

F –

G –

H –

I –

J –

K –

L –

M –

N –

O –

P –

Q –

R –

S –

T –

U –

V –

W –

X –

Y –

Z –

Results

How many different things did you find?
Write your results down here! How much did you
score out of 26?

/ 26

Scoring system

5 or fewer – Try harder!

6-15 – Good work!

16-25 – Excellent!

26 – FULL HOUSE!!!! Way to go, brainbox!

Conclusion

Insects, bugs and creepy crawlies come in all different shapes and sizes. It's important to have a wide variety of creatures on the planet so that there's lots of biodiversity. Everything in nature is interdependent, which means we all need each other: humans need plants and animals and creepy crawlies, otherwise the whole system would break down. For instance, bees are really important as they help flowering plants reproduce. We even need fungus and bacteria to help break down dead and decaying matter and to return the nutrients to the soil so the cycle of life can repeat. Without them we wouldn't exist! We have to preserve the habitats of each and every living thing on our planet.

EXPERIMENT TO SHOW HOW THE FIRE TRIANGLE WORKS!

Fire is AWESOME! It looks so pretty — I could watch it all day. But, because I'm at primary school, I'm only allowed to use it with a parent or guardian present. Luckily, it's for my own health and safety. Whatever you do, please do NOT attempt this experiment without a grown-up.

Materials

matches · saucer · jam jar · water

Method

Light a match and place it on your saucer. Put the jam jar on top of the match and the flame will go out because you've taken away the oxygen.

I can't breathe! I'm suffocating!

Light another match and place it on the saucer again.

This time don't do anything. Once the matchstick has burnt out so it's black and shrivelled, the flame will disappear because the fuel (the wood of the matchstick) has all been used up.

Help! I'm disappearing!

Now pour some water on your saucer. Light another match and place it on the wet saucer.

The flame will go out again because the water has taken away all the heat!

Help! I'm drowning!

Results

The three things that fire needs are heat, oxygen and fuel.

Fuel – this can be gas like some cookers use or coal like in a fireplace or wood as

Fuel e.g. logs
Don't use my log though!

with our wooden match. Remove it and your fire goes out like when you turn your cooker off and the gas is taken away.

Oxygen – fire burns well in open air as 20 per cent of our air is oxygen (just in case you were

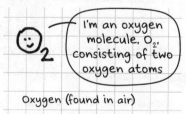
I'm an oxygen molecule, O_2, consisting of two oxygen atoms
Oxygen (found in air)

wondering, the other 78 per cent is nitrogen, 0.04 per cent is carbon dioxide, and the rest is made up of inert gases).

This is why if you smother a fire by putting a

blanket over it then it will go out.

My dad's restaurant even has fire blankets in the kitchen just for putting out fires. By covering a fire, its oxygen supply is cut off and it's basically suffocated.

Heat – fire needs to be hot to thrive. This is why throwing enough cold water over a fire will usually put it out – you've taken away the heat.

Heat – did you know a wood fire can exceed 1100°C?

It's the best method for putting out big fires that you can't 'suffocate' easily, like forest fires, which are sometimes tackled by spraying water over the top of them from an aeroplane.

Conclusion

A fire needs fuel, oxygen

and heat to burn! Without any one of these three things, you can't make a fire!

HOW TO MAKE A CAMPFIRE HASH, COOKIE-STYLE!

This is a variation of the breakfast we ate when we were camping. It serves four children. Maybe me, Jake and Keziah could come round and help you eat it! Remember, you should only make this recipe with a parent or guardian!

YUM!

Materials

Frying pan – (my mum has a really heavy one but for little wrists like ours it might be better to use a light one so the food doesn't jump out of the frying pan and into the fire – that's a phrase that grown-ups use for when things go from bad to worse!)

Wooden spoon – (I hope your hash tastes as nice as when I make it, otherwise I'll win first prize and you'll get the wooden spoon!)

One medium onion, chopped – (here's a good tip – if you bite a metal spoon when you chop onions it will stop you from crying. It works because the chemicals from the onion bind to the metal of the spoon before they can get to your eyes!)

A tablespoon of cooking oil – (my mum makes me drink a teaspoon of cod liver oil every day – it's really good for your bones, your heart, your vision and your brain apparently, but it's definitely not good for cooking with! My worst oil is palm oil because palm trees are being cut down to make it, destroying the habitat of the orang-utans. Always use sustainable palm oil.)

A garlic clove, minced – (garlic is good for warding off vampires apparently, although I don't believe in vampires or ghosts as you know!

Alison Denbigh probably does . . .)

279

500g new potatoes, quartered –
(if you keep the skin on them then
you'll get loads of fibre, as that's
where all their fibre comes from.)

4–6 sausages, sliced into discs –
(you can use veggie sausages too if you're a
vegetarian like I want to be when I grow up.)

A can of sweetcorn – (if you don't have sweetcorn you
could use any chopped frozen veg knocking about in your
freezer. Frozen veg is really healthy because it's frozen
quickly after it's been picked so will remain at its peak
in terms of freshness and nutrients. If a vegetable isn't
frozen then its nutrients reduce over time as it gets
less fresh, which is why it's good to pick
veg that hasn't travelled very far. Not only
is seasonal local produce usually fresher
but it has a lower carbon footprint too!

Method

Pour the oil into
the frying pan.

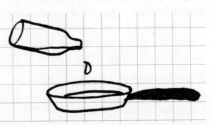

Once the oil is
warm, fry your
chopped onion and
garlic. Add the potatoes and
cook for twenty minutes,
stirring occasionally. The
smaller the potato pieces
are, the quicker they'll cook!

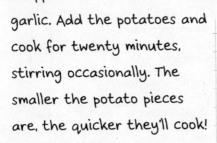

Add the sliced sausage and stir for another
10–15 minutes until the potatoes are tender and
golden, and the sausages are cooked through. Mix
in the corn until all of it is
heated well.

Results

Yummy!

Conclusion

It's good but would be even better served with
baked beans and sprinkled with salt and pepper!

COOKIE!

in her mysterious next adventure!

Turn the page
for a sneak peek
at my new story!

COOKIE!

...and the MOST MYSTERIOUS
MYSTERY in the WORLD

OUT IN AUGUST 2021

CHAPTER 1

Secrets

Why is it that parents always say 'nothing' when you ask them questions about their conversations with other grown-ups?

What's a flexible mortgage?

Nothing

It's like they think we're being nosy or that we're too young to understand things. But how can we learn anything if they don't tell us stuff?

What's the meaning of life, Mummy?

Nothing

Oh

A good way to learn things in life is to ask questions, but 'nothing' is NOT a good answer!

What does it mean, 'Mrs Miggins gave our milkman a hickey?'

Nothing

I suppose there are a few exceptions . . .

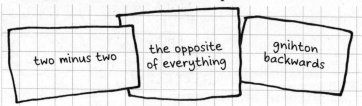

two minus two

the opposite of everything

gnihton backwards

Today, my mum got a letter from my Nani (her mum) in Bangladesh and spent a good twenty minutes reading it and laughing out loud like it was the funniest joke book ever written.

ha ha

hee hee

ho ho

When I asked her what it said she just kept saying 'nothing'.

'*Nothing* doesn't make people laugh,' I replied.

And she said, 'Really it's nothing . . . just Nani being Nani.' Well, that's even more ridiculous! Of course Nani is being Nani! Who else would she be? Father Christmas?! Now that would be weird.

Nani, is that you?

Ho ho ho . . . merry Xmas!

Saying 'Nani is just being Nani' is a tautology. A tautology is when you repeat something that's already been implied in the same sentence, like the scorching sun was boiling hot. Well of course it's boiling hot or it wouldn't be scorching!!!

Or calling a mystery mysterious! That's a tautology. Of course mysteries are mysterious. Duh!

Unlike most other people at school, I hardly know my nani cos she lives in Bangladesh. I've only been there once and although it was for the whole of the summer holidays I was just a baby so I don't even remember it.

Nani is Bengali for a gran that's your mum's mum.

My nani lives in a small village in Bangladesh. She
doesn't even have Skype or a mobile phone so every
now and then Mum gets these
really long letters updating
her on the family back home
and all the village goings-on.
Judging by the amount Mum
laughs, the letters seem to be

funnier than a stand-up comedy routine.

Maybe if Nani lived here she could
be a comedian. I like to think I've
inherited her genetics and that I'm
quite funny too.

Genetics are the coding handed down in our
DNA that give us our inherited family characteristics.

Talking of coding, I wish I could read Bengali.
After Mum had finished reading Nani's letter, she
left it on the kitchen counter. I tried to have a look

5

but it was like a foreign language to me . . . probably because it was, I guess. Bengali looks really cool written down. It all hangs off a line and is in neat shapes. I already know how to write my name . . .

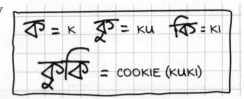

My sisters can write their names as well – my mum taught all of us how to do it as soon as we could pick up a pen.

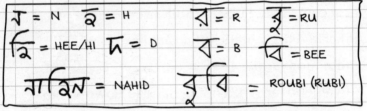

I was only a few months old when we went to Bangladesh but my sisters came back speaking Bengali really well and now it's like everyone in my family can speak in code except for me.

My eldest sister, Nahid, speaks it better than Roubi, my middle sister. I can hardly speak it at all – I only know three words.

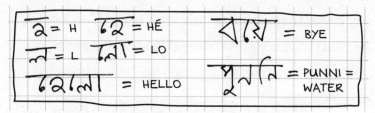

But I like to think they're three really important

words . . .

Clement Boudin in our
year at school can speak
FOUR different languages.

1. French: he was born there and

his parents are French.

 2. English: he moved to England in
Year Two and picked up English

within a few months.

3. Spanish: his childminder spoke to

him in Spanish so he learnt it from her.

4. Russian: yep! Russian!! His mum's parents are

 Russian and they taught him it. He could

be an interpreter and work for MI5!

Imagine speaking FOUR languages! How cool is that?! Apparently, babies can learn hundreds of different languages . . .

Each language uses only about 40 sounds or 'phonemes', which distinguish one language from another. At birth the baby brain has an unusual gift: it can tell the difference between all 800 sounds. This means that infants can learn any language they're exposed to . . .

Can you repeat that in French for me? I prefer speaking French at home

Merçi!

I decide to bike over to Keziah's. I love having my new bike – it's so brilliant being able to see Keziah whenever I like.

Where's she going this late? It's 3 a.m.!

As I'm leaving the house, Jake, who lives next door, is finishing off washing his mum's car and decides to tag along.

'Hey, Jake! How come you're washing the car again? You only just did it last week!'

'Mum keeps making excuses to get me out the house,' he explains. 'Not only have I washed the car twice today, but I've mowed the lawn AND been

to the shops three times to pick
things up for her. It's so odd.
She'll probably be over the moon
that I'm going to Keziah's with
you. She's acting so weird and
being really mysterious.'

'Let me guess,' I reply. 'When you try to get to the
bottom of it, she just says it's "nothing", right?'

'Right!' he says.

Why are parents so
complicated sometimes?
Why all the secrecy? We're
old enough to be trusted
with stuff at our age.

At Keziah's, her dads,
Mal and Paul, are having a few people over to watch
the football on the telly. They're laughing lots and
keep talking about 'that time at White Hart Lane'.
The three of us head up to Keziah's bedroom.

'What's White Hart Lane?' I ask.

'A football stadium,' replies Keziah. 'They're
always laughing about "that time at White Hart
Lane under the bleachers" but no one will tell me
what they're talking about.'

'Bleachers are the seats that are tiered or raised in rows like stairs,' says Jake.

'I know that but I'm still none the wiser,' Keziah sighs. 'I think it's got something to do with me.'

Keziah's room is in the loft so it has sloping ceilings and skylights you can look out of and nosy at the whole street undetected! It's really cool and good for spying. It's a bit like being in a secret hideaway in the roof. Keziah loves drawing and her whole room is covered in artwork – in fact, the whole house is! Paul and Mal have framed her drawings and hung them everywhere and some of them look really professional.

'Heyyyy! Look what I've got,' says Jake, pulling a brand-new Z-Box 3 Pro out of his backpack.

'No way! You're not even into gaming! How come you've got one of those?' I ask, trying to hide my jealousy. I love gaming but can only dream of

my owning my own
Z-Box 3 Pro.

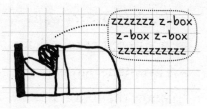

'I know, right?' says
Jake. 'My mum got
it for me out of the blue and I've no idea why. She
keeps getting me presents.'

We start to formulate theories behind Jake's
mum's sudden generosity, secrecy and general
weirdness. Keziah reckons she
might have an online gambling
habit.

'She probably needs you out
of the house so she can go on the laptop and log on
to the cyber casino without you knowing,' she says.

'But why all the gifts?' asks Jake.

'Maybe she buys you stuff with her winnings out
of guilt,' I chip in.

'Not a bad explanation,' replies Jake. 'Although it
doesn't explain why she's being extra nice to me.'

'Maybe she's trying to make up for the fact that
your dad's moved out?' suggests Keziah.

I wonder what Jake's mum's hiding.
Keziah is brilliant at keeping secrets.
I would trust her with my life.

She's almost too good at it. One time, Axel Kahn told her that he'd seen Mr Hastings, our deputy head, and Miss Rai, one of the reception teachers, in Nando's together, sitting in the corner behind a pillar!!!

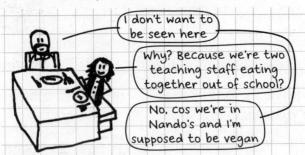

Keziah didn't even tell *me* cos Axel made her promise not to tell anyone. Not even ME?!! Come on, Keziah!! I've no idea why it was such a big deal in the first place, two teachers eating chicken . . . hardly a classified state secret.

I only found out when Axel accidentally mentioned it to me. Anyway, if it *was* supposed to be a secret, why go somewhere as popular as Nando's?

But the point is . . . KEZIAH DIDN'T TELL ME!!

She said it's because
Axel made her swear
on her life. I was really
annoyed. I think she's
learnt her lesson –
we tell each other
everything now.

Does make you wonder though, was it some sort
of staff meeting or is something
else going on? What did they
chat about? School? Teaching
methods? Their undying love
for each other?

My eldest sister, Nahid, is the WORST at keeping
secrets – like the time she told Dad I'd made a
woodlouse farm in a shoe
box that I kept hidden
in the corner of my
bedroom . . .

AND the time she told Dad
I'd stolen a cola bottle from
the pick and mix . . .

AND the time she told Mum *and* Dad that I pretended my cardigan was a pet cat . . .

After we finish playing on the Z-Box, Keziah shows us how to make a coding wheel.

A coding wheel is basically two circles of card with the alphabet written on them, and you set the circles so that each letter of the alphabet corresponds to a totally different letter. You can then code messages to send to each other.

UNCODE THIS:
TALZKJ
UGFV

We all decide to make one so we can send each other secret messages. We code and decode messages until it's time to go home.

When I get back there's an ambulance parked outside my house. What on earth is going on?

My dad and Roubi are standing on the pavement and a few other neighbours are gathered around too, including Jake's mum.

The ambulance drives off. Huh?

'What's going on?' I ask.

'Get in the car,' says Dad. 'Your sister's been in an accident. We need to go to the hospital.'

Thank you for choosing a Piccadilly Press book.

If you would like to know more about our
authors or our books, or if you'd just like to know
what we're up to, you can find us online.

www.piccadillypress.co.uk

And you can also find us on:

We hope to see you soon!